WHEN
LOVE
ABOUNDS

Sloane Patterson,
May God's abounding love
surround and keep you.

Blessings,
Linda Robinson

WHEN LOVE ABOUNDS

*a novel of faith,
hope, and love*

LINDA ROBINSON

TATE PUBLISHING & *Enterprises*

When Love Abounds
Copyright © 2010 by Linda Robinson. All rights reserved.

Scriptures taken from the Holy Bible, New International Version®, NIV®. Copyright © 1973, 1978, 1984 by Biblica, Inc.™ Used by permission of Zondervan. All rights reserved worldwide. www.zondervan.com

This book is a work of fiction. Names, characters, places, and incidents are the product of the author's imagination or are used fictitiously. Any resemblance to actual events, locals, or persons, living or dead, is coincidental.

The opinions expressed by the author are not necessarily those of Tate Publishing, LLC.

Published by Tate Publishing & Enterprises, LLC
127 E. Trade Center Terrace | Mustang, Oklahoma 73064 USA
1.888.361.9473 | www.tatepublishing.com

Tate Publishing is committed to excellence in the publishing industry. The company reflects the philosophy established by the founders, based on Psalm 68:11,
"The Lord gave the word and great was the company of those who published it."

Book design copyright © 2010 by Tate Publishing, LLC. All rights reserved.
Cover design by Amber Gulilat
Interior design by Joey Garrett

Published in the United States of America

ISBN: 978-1-61663-882-5
1. Fiction / Christian / General
2. Fiction / Family Life
10.08.23

DEDICATION

First, I want to thank you, my husband, Bruce, for your unwavering support and encouragement—not just while I was writing this book, but throughout all our years together. You gave and continue to give me strength and courage and much more. A simple "I love you" seems enormously inadequate. I dedicate this book to you, my love.

To my immediate family: Timothy, Katie, Kenneth, Kelly, Nathaniel, Marilee, Chris, Preston, Joshua, Harold, Mandy, Trish, Mike, Mikey, Jayden, Kathie, Sandy, and Christopher ... I love all of you, and I pray God will bless you all abundantly.

To my brother, Bob: I love you much! May God bless you.

To the memory of my father, David, who grounded me in faith.

Lastly, I want to dedicate this book to the memory of my dear friend, Tammy, who sadly did not live to see it published. Tammy will always be one of my most cherished mentors, a neighbor for many years, a coworker for four years, and my friend throughout eternity.

ACKNOWLEDGMENTS

I thank my heavenly Father for giving me the vision, the courage, and the ability to complete the sometimes daunting task of writing this book. His love amazes me.

To my dear friends Nancy L., Vanessa O., Janice, Mamie, and Leila: without your encouragement, ideas, suggestions, and all other inputs during the early stages of this project, you might not be holding this book in your hands—at least not in the present form. Janice, you deserve an extra special thank you for reading my final draft on such short notice. Thank you, Elaine, for proof reading for me ... also on short notice. Your expertise and experience through years of teaching high school English and literature helped me tremendously. God put all of you in my life for a reason. I love and thank you all.

Cindy Kelley, I can't possibly express the extent of my gratitude to you in these few short sentences. Thank you for taking time from your busy schedule to read my manuscript, make suggestions, give me tips to help me self-edit ... and for offering kind words of encouragement when my confidence often waned. When we worked together over three decades ago, I never dreamed we'd one day reconnect in this line of work. Your diverse talents overwhelm me. I pray God will bless you in all your endeavors, and you'll have many more years of successful writing. Unforgettable story of a mother's unconditional love aside, the imagery alone in *The Silent Gift* blew me away!

I would like to thank the entire staff at Tate Publishing, with a special thanks to those I worked closely with during this process: my editor, Emily Wilson; cover designer, Amber Gulilat; and layout designer, Joey Garrett. Last but not least, I'd like to thank Stacy Baker, who started it all.

FOREWORD

*W*hen *Love Abounds* is a story Linda Robinson felt compelled to write. Much like her protagonist, Lou Ellen Newman, Linda felt something pulling her—nudging her to share her faith in her own unique way—to write a novel that portrays the truth of how God is there to carry each of us through all the times of our life.

It's no small feat to put a story down on paper—to start at the beginning, work your way through the middle, and come up with an ending that makes readers feel like they've just spent their time wisely. Yet Linda Robinson has done that by writing a character we immediately like in the beginning of the book, root for through the middle, and grow to love in the end.

In a day and age when technology is supposed to lessen our time doing daily tasks, it seems that we're busier than ever. Most of us lead hectic lives filled to the brim with endless errands, worries, and obligations. We could all take a lesson from Lou Ellen in *When Love Abounds* and stop the busyness long enough to feed the birds, appreciate the beauty of the flowers, and love the view from our own front and back porches.

—Cindy Kelley, screenwriter of *The Velveteen Rabbit* and *Love Comes Softly*, co-author of *The Silent Gift*

And now these three remain: faith, hope and love. And the greatest of these is love.

1 Corinthians 13:13 (NIV)

PART ONE

LOOKING FOR LOVE

CHAPTER ONE

DEEP IN THE HEART OF DIXIE—
SPRINGTIME, 2007

Valley Lake was a small, quaint city so widespread and picturesque that it appeared to have been sprinkled into the landscape between the rivers, lakes, and streams by some fairy darting about just overhead, using her sparkling wand to create businesses and houses wherever there was dry land. In summer the picture was completed when she returned to paint borders with fields of cotton, peanuts, and corn, fringing the pastures of black and white cows. Churches dotted every corner and then some. If it had been *her* choice, Lou Ellen might have named it Peaceful, Alabama.

Tonight, all the signs were evident . . . it was spring, her favorite time of year. The air felt cool but refreshing as she stood leaning against one of the large white columns on the long veranda. With a pleased sigh, she inhaled the sweet scent of the native azaleas blooming outside. The quietness of the midnight hour was periodically interrupted by the cacophony of crickets, katydids, or cicadas in the surrounding trees, and a choir of pond frogs in the water nearby. Rather than dissonant, it was melodious to her—nature's symphony. Occasionally, the bass croak of a bullfrog resonated from the far side of the pond, completing the masterpiece. *How I love this place!* she thought.

Aided by the light of the full moon, she glimpsed the ghostly silhouette of the red fox as he slinked past her line of vision on his mission to the yard cats' food bowls. She kept her eyes on him as she crept quietly across the tiled patio and passed the last column to watch him through the windows of the outdoor kitchen. He quickly ate and then disappeared into the shadows of the redbud and magnolia trees.

She and her husband, Burt, had first spied his bushy tail at dusk one evening while they sat on the screened lanai, taking time out to talk and enjoy the relaxing babble of the fountain and watch the birds feeding or taking baths. He'd been snooping around the bird feeding station, which she kept filled with not only birdseed, but where she placed various stale breads, cakes, potato chips, and other snacks on the tray. She had scattered portions on the ground for the doves and other ground feeding birds, and Little Red, as she'd named him, had found it. Her motto had always been, "When life gives you crumbs… feed the birds, when life gives you prosperity… feed the birds, in *any* life… just feed the birds." *They ate well.*

Simply put, the estate catered to a myriad of wildlife, and she enjoyed them all… with the exception of perhaps too many deer, which ate more than their share of her flowers and shrubs. Due to their voracious appetites, many plants had to be fenced to survive at all. She had quickly learned which plants could survive *only* if planted in the indoor flower garden, protected by the domed screen of the lanai.

It had become quite a challenge to keep enough food available to feed all the little critters, as she referred to them. Opossums and raccoons most likely ate more cat food than the cats and often absconded with the entire suet cake *and* the wire cage that held it on the shelf of the bird feeder. She never figured out how they were able to get the chain free that fastened the suet holder to the post. *They must be little Houdini varmints,* she thought.

Wild turkeys often sashayed across the pond dam on their meandering path to the base of the bird feeder. Colorful wood ducks and mallards frequented the ponds and paddled around in circles at approximately the same time and place every afternoon, waiting for her to appear with the food she tossed into the water… food they had to share with the catfish, blue gill, and shell cracker brim.

If she *had* to choose a favorite of all the birds, it would be the hummingbirds. She prepared literally gallons of nectar for them every year. She once had so many hummingbird feeders hanging in the trees and sitting on the windowsills that she thought she needed to hire a helper, because she and Burt could no longer keep up with the maintenance of so many. So she downsized. Besides, they had plenty to eat in their own flower garden, which was filled with only the plants that produced flowers humming-birds enjoyed most. They dined from their own smorgasbord of fire-bush, red-hot poker, shrimp plant, salvia, purple coneflower, Turk's cap, and many more. From inside the house, she could move in close to the window, stand motionless, and watch—up close and personal—as they perched and ate from the window feeders. With their long and skinny tongues, they flicked out drops of sweet nectar onto the window ledge as they brought it back to their bills to drink. She could see their tiny throats as they appeared to be gargling. The splattered nectar on the sill attracted gnats and other minute flying insects, resulting in addi-tional food for the hummers.

One summer, pre-wild cat days, a cottontail rabbit raised her babies in the flowerbed just outside the front door. The doe dug a hole, pulled hair from her body to line the nest before giving birth, and covered the nest with pine straw and leaves any time she left the babies alone. Through the window Lou Ellen often watched the doe come to the flowerbed and stretch out across the bed to allow her babies to nurse. As they got older, any slight noise or movement near the nest signaled the babies to come wiggling up out of their furry, leafy baby bed … probably think-ing Mama was home and it was dinnertime!

Wrens built nests in the most bizarre places, and the garage door had to be kept closed in spring and summer to prevent the birds entering the garage to build nests in a shoe, hanging flow-erpot, or straw hat. It had happened quite often, but it posed a problem in that the garage door had to be left partially raised until the babies fledged. Snakes loved that! It had only taken one incident of opening the door from the laundry room into the garage, encountering a snake slithering across the floor, and she had banned the birds—forever.

One of her favorite memories was of a nest of bluebird babies just outside the veranda in the nesting box Burt had built for her enjoyment. While having their morning coffee each day, she and Burt watched the male and female catching insects and constantly feeding them for over two weeks. After the babies fledged, she noticed the parents continued to look for bugs and worms to take to the babies perched in the trees. So she had an idea.

She went to the bait and tackle store and bought a bucket of live crickets. Twice every day she took it down under the trees, called to the babies, and threw some crickets out. At first only the adult birds came, grabbed the crickets, and flew back to the trees and fed them. Soon the fledglings began flying to the ground *with* them—when they heard Lou Ellen calling.

Before long Burt became interested in watching too. One day two of the babies grabbed the same cricket, and for a few seconds they had a tug-of-war over whose delicious dinner it was going to be. But all too soon, the parents forced their young to be on their own to fend for themselves.

On their own to fend for themselves... the thought evoked elusive, sketchy bits and pieces of a memory that threatened to assault her! *Why can't I bring it back... clearly? Could it be I don't really want to remember?*

Suddenly she heard the haunting howl of a wild coyote up in the pecan orchard, jarring her mind back to the present. It was not her favorite sound, nor did she have any fondness for coyotes. She wondered if they could be responsible for the disappearance of the brood of adorable wood duck babies in the pond, which had steadily diminished by one or two every night... until there were none left.

Beside her favorite chair on the veranda, she kept a pair of night-vision goggles to watch the creatures who ventured into the yard, along with binoculars for checking out the different species of birds at the feeder during the day. Seeing those visual aids now reminded her of something she needed to mention to

Ralph, their gardener. She'd noticed the gardenia bush was getting too large—partially blocking her view of the bird feeder—so it needed to be pruned.

Ralph was such a blessing. He'd told her he loved working the estate, and she knew he was a tremendous help to Burt, who admitted *he* mostly just loved his vegetable gardening hobby these days. He said he grew gardens just for the fun of *growing* and the joy of *sharing* with others. He said "dirt-digging" was just in his *blood* ... in his *DNA*. But she often saw Burt and Ralph working side by side, laughing and talking together, doing *all* the chores. Ralph was quiet, a man of few words, and when he was amused he'd just smile or let out a barely audible chuckle. But Burt could make him laugh so hard his body shook. He'd throw his head back, and you could hear the pleasant sounds rumbling from his belly up as laughter exploded in a howl. It was one of those laughs that made *her* laugh too—the contagious kind.

Ralph and his wife, Cecily, had been employed as their gardener and housekeeper for ten years. They had both been born and raised in the Deep South, had spent twenty years away while Ralph was in the military, and then moved back home. Cecily had grown up without a father and had not gotten a formal education, but she had a heart of gold and loved life. She and Lou Ellen had become dear friends. Two years ago she and Ralph had a run of financial bad luck due to medical problems, and Burt had moved them into the guest house on their land, which was nestled among the trees and shrubs near one of the ponds. They were not merely *employees;* they were like family—very special people.

Lou Ellen could hear Burt's soft, peaceful snore as he lay sleeping just inside the double doors from which she'd emerged. When weather permitted, she often came out here at night if she was having trouble sleeping. Only yesterday she'd told Cecily how peaceful it was out here after the whole countryside went to bed. Cecily had looked aghast.

"Lordy, Miz Lou, ain't you scared to be out yonder on that big ol' porch all by yo'self come dark? It just ain't safe, you know!" she said, her eyes round as saucers.

Overhearing the conversation, Burt turned to her and said, "Rest assured of one thing, Cee, if anybody ever gets the nerve to snatch Miz Lou off the porch and take her away, they'll surely bring her back—a lot faster than they took her!"

Cecily cackled with amusement. "Umm ... Mr. B, you better watch yo back. You've put yo foot in yo mouth now ... Miz Lou'll get even with you for that!"

Lou Ellen smiled and gave Cecily a wink of conspiracy while forming a circle with her thumb and forefinger, which tickled Cecily even more.

Burt was good at keeping Cecily entertained. Mischief lurked behind the perpetual twinkle in his eyes. *The cheeky pot-stirring troublemaker!* she thought with a smile on her face.

She certainly was *not* afraid out here. It was her cherished, private, personal time—time to talk to God, to thank him. It was time when she thanked him for her present station in life, and time when she sometimes reflected on her past, a past where time seemingly stood still, and a present where time was flying—truly a paradox.

Her life had not always been like this ... peaceful, joyful and fulfilling, with her every need supplied. While certainly not wealthy now by the world's standards, without question she had been most richly blessed. There was a time early on when she couldn't or wouldn't remember much about her pre-Burt life. She just knew that, unlike Burt, her childhood had not been a care-free, happy one. *Did I ever really have a childhood—by the normal definition of the word?*

But now she could re-visit most of those unhappy times, and with God's help, she could understand them and wasn't bitter—nor had she ever been bitter. Now she could understand her dys-functional family better and why she, as well as others, was a victim. At least she didn't purposely block certain events from her memory anymore. In spite of, or *because* of them, she felt she was more forgiving and understanding; and she loved and cared about others. It was all because of God's marvelous love and grace—and Burt.

Recently, however, her thoughts seemed to wander more and more frequently to her past. She felt a yen, a desire just beyond her ability to define, an elusive feeling of something unfinished, something she couldn't quite wrap her mind around, as though maybe she needed to *do* something. *But... what?* She felt an overwhelming need to pray, to say, "Lord, if there is something I haven't done, or something I need to do, tell me... show me... please just give me a sign." So she prayed.

Slowly, like the fluffy soft layers of cotton candy clouds unfurled by a crisp spring breeze, one by one the memories began floating by, some of which she could grasp for only a few short seconds. Others, unbidden, disturbing, and undefined scuttled past... so close, yet just out of reach. And she gladly let those go.

Just a hint of cool breeze stirred the short tentacles of chestnut hair framing her forehead and cheeks, as if to caress her face and whisper her name. With a half pleasant, half uneasy sigh, gradually her mind began to focus—to walk among the memories...

CHAPTER TWO

S he was sitting in the high chair beside the long table with lots of food. Her dishwater blonde, stringy hair was straggling around her chubby two-year-old face and lying limp and hot about her shoulders. She could see her "big brudder" sitting at the table with lots of other little boys and girls.

Someone put a glass of milk on her tray. When she reached for the glass, one of the kids at the table distracted her, and she knocked it over—filling her tray with the cold, sweet liquid. As she stared down at the milk, one of the adults all the kids were calling Sweetie came stomping over to her. She was mad. She was yelling! Loudly!

"Lou Ellen, for crying out loud! Can't you just pay attention to what you're doing? What is wrong with you? Now you just lick every drop of that milk off that tray, right now! Do you hear me, young lady? Go on. Now! Lap it up!" The other kids were laughing…

Why can I remember that so vividly? It must have been embarrassing, but how so, at such a young age?

That night she was put to bed with lots of other little girls, all of them with their feet toward the center of the bed. When she got up in the morning, Sweetie took care of her and all the other girls. One pretty girl with long blonde hair cried a lot, and Sweetie picked her up, sat her on her lap, held her close, and rocked her. That happened often, but *not* for Lou Ellen.

She wondered if she had been too young to understand, if she'd been jealous, and if she had misbehaved. She couldn't remember ever getting a spanking there. Try as she might, she just could not remember *any* other details. The only thing she knew for sure was that Sweetie had rejected her, and it was declared through the perpetual scowl on her face when she looked at her and the stern tone of her disapproving voice when she spoke to her.

Oh yes! The soft and cuddly puppy the one that we held while we let him drink a tiny, warm bottle of milk! We argued over who was going to hold him while he drank his dinner like a baby. The man who lived there made us all take turns and share in feeding him.

Even as young as she was, she had been allowed her turn too. Oh, how much she'd loved that sweet puppy's breath and kisses! And that was her first childhood memory—not of being loved *herself*, but of loving and caring for that precious dog. It was hungry, and *she* had fed it.

CHAPTER THREE

Lou Ellen. Her name used to be Lou Ellen *Hudson*. Her birth certificate, issued back in 1941, had read Lou Ella. Her daddy, Daniel, said that was wrong, so she'd changed it when she got older. Her daddy said she was born at home. Home was a small, unpainted shanty with no indoor plumbing or electricity, with plank walls and floorboards, some with wide cracks through which cold wind blew in winter and mosquitoes and other bugs crawled in summer. He said he paid a midwife $6 to assist in the delivery, and he had to borrow that from his sister and brother-in-law.

Her brother, Nathan, was three years old when she was born. She was told she was a beautiful baby with blonde hair, big blue eyes, and a quick, wide smile. Without pictures, she had no idea. Her one and only baby picture was a yellowed black and white snapshot, taken of her standing outdoors when she was around twelve months of age—compliments of her Grandmother Hudson many years later. The words *baby's first steps* were written on the back in her grandmother's scratchy handwriting.

Lou Ellen was told her biological mother, Mary, was a beautiful woman and was very young when Nathan was born. Allegedly, one day Mary secured the skirt of Lou Ellen's dress underneath the leg of the old iron poster bed, left her and Nathan at home alone, and ran away with an army soldier. They had a wreck, the soldier was decapitated, and her mother was hospitalized with severe disfiguring facial lacerations. Daniel visited Mary in the hospital, told her he would take her back, but she refused and asked for a divorce—and gave *him* the kids. Lou Ellen was between one and two years of age then, but no one seemed to know her exact age. They said it was the same year her daddy lost his own father, whom he idolized. He couldn't handle so many traumas, had a mental breakdown, and was subsequently institutionalized. Hence, the foster home for Nathan and her at some point thereafter.

Since her limited source of information had always been from someone in her daddy's family, Lou Ellen had to give her mother the benefit of the doubt—cut her some slack. One relative had even hinted that her mother and daddy were having problems and were living apart even when her brother was born. But she never could find a relative who knew—or would tell—the whole story. She thought it just possibly could have been that her daddy had a breakdown, her mother couldn't handle it ... so she left.

Even so, does that justify leaving one's children behind, alone, to fend for themselves?

Lou Ellen had been told Mary was raised by a couple who were not even relatives of hers. She thought maybe her mother hadn't known any genuine love herself, as a child. *Or ... was she simply lacking in mothering instincts?* she wondered. *So many questions and so few answers!*

Lou Ellen was never told how long she and Nathan lived in the foster home or, for that matter, their exact ages when they were taken there; but eventually Daniel came and took them home. She didn't know if it was the same house her mother had shared with them before she left. Her name was never mentioned at home. Relatives had told Lou Ellen that her grandmother and different aunts and uncles took turns and kept Nathan and her quite often—pre and post foster home—at least on the days their daddy worked. He worked as a common laborer, riding a bicycle to and from work, if or when he could find anything to do. The world was at war, food was rationed, and jobs were extremely hard to come by. Most of the aunts and uncles already had large families of their own. *Bet that was a thrill a minute—two more kids to feed and care for when it was already a challenge to provide enough food for their own in those tough times,* she thought.

Daniel had to transport her and her brother by bicycle to and from the relative who happened to be keeping them for him on any given day. All roads were country dirt roads through farmland, and the relatives lived miles apart; so a lot of her daddy's workday was used to travel to and from babysitters. He'd once described to her how he'd positioned two sleepy children on the bike with him—even before daylight sometimes, in order to get them to the sitter and then get to work on time. Her brother said he could remember, but she couldn't recall any of those arduous trips.

While the three of them were living alone, Lou Ellen became sick with fever and sore throat, and her daddy put her to bed. That same day some of his sisters came to visit, brought them some apples, and gave Lou Ellen one; however, her daddy took it, cut it in half, and gave half of it back to her. She threw a crying tantrum, threw the apple across the room, and he spanked her on the leg. She remembered it well—it broke her heart. Her aunts got mad at Daniel and told him that since Lou Ellen was sick he shouldn't spank her, but he didn't agree. She'd learned a valuable lesson that day—her daddy did not tolerate any tantrum-throwing sessions … sick or well.

Daniel taught Nathan and Lou Ellen about Jesus, gave them each a tiny New Testament Bible, and taught them to pray the well-known children's prayers: the "God is good, God is great …" and the "Now I lay me down to sleep …" ones. Though she couldn't read yet, Lou Ellen loved her "Bibie" and wouldn't go to bed without it. Instead of a *blankie,* she had a *Bibie,* which she covered with both hands and held underneath her chin before going to sleep. She remembered her daddy taught her to sing "Jesus Wuvs Me." *Later on I had a profound need to remember the words to that song—for strength and comfort in my darkest moments,* she thought.

Lou Ellen's next recollections began when she was three and a half years of age. They'd moved again—still in the country, but *near* the town of Cloverton and miles away from her aunts and uncles. Since her Granddaddy Hudson had passed away when she was a toddler, her grandmother came to live with them for a little while, to take care of them while their daddy worked. She was a godly woman who read her Bible and prayed daily. She was strict but good to them, and she and Nathan loved her.

One night when Daniel was late coming home from work, Grandmother Hudson cooked supper, and the three of them sat down to eat. Like the shanty Lou Ellen was born in, their house had no electricity. It was dark, and the oil lamp was lit and sitting in the middle of the small kitchen table. She and Nathan had always been prone to get tickled at the supper table, which was an absolute no-no when their daddy was home. So, they took a quick mischievous look at each other and immediately burst out laughing. Lou Ellen had just taken a big swallow of cold chocolate milk, which she spewed over the hot glass shade of the lamp . . . causing it to shatter.

Oops . . . big, b-i-g trouble—spanking time! She remembered thinking.

But their grandmother didn't spank them. She gave them a flashlight and made them take the broken pieces of glass out to a deep gully behind their house and toss them over. That was okay with Lou Ellen; but her brother, being terribly afraid of the dark, told her he would much rather *have a beating!*

CHAPTER FOUR

When Lou Ellen had just turned four years old, Daniel told her and her brother he was going to bring home a new mother for them. Since she had never known one, Lou Ellen didn't know what to expect, but she was excited. She and Nathan had never even met her. When their grandmother told them one morning the day had finally arrived, they waited outside and anxiously watched for them to come, talking to each other and wondering—what would she look like? Be like? What would she say to them?

It wasn't long before their daddy arrived with his new bride, and he told them that her name was Lena, but they were going to call her "Mother." Lena brought each of them a gift—a slab of coconut candy made of different colored stripes. Lou Ellen thought it was the prettiest candy she had ever seen—and the best thing she had ever eaten! She didn't have any other memories of that day, except one. It was the day their grandmother left. She went to live with one of their aunts, and she and Nathan were sad to see her go. *Another significant mother figure disappeared from their lives.*

Lou Ellen didn't know exactly when or why they moved there, but they were living out in the country in a small log cabin within walking distance of her new mother's family, the Simpsons. She didn't know it at the time, but Lena was twenty-five years old when she and Daniel married, hadn't been married before, and was never comfortable away from her own mother. *My daddy probably moved there to make his new wife happy,* she thought. *It seemed it was his goal in life—to make Lena happy. He never gave up trying.*

Her mother took her and Nathan to Granny Simpson's house every day, walking the winding and narrow dirt road that ambled through the woods and across a small babbling brook. Their Granny and Gramps Simpson were good to them. Granny was a good cook, and they never went hungry. To Lou Ellen, the Simpsons seemed like a large family. Besides her mother, they had five grown sons and daughters still living at home, so there were seven of them already, plus her mother, her brother, and her most of the time too. They ate their dinner *and* supper there, stayed until nearly dark every day, and then walked back to their log cabin to sleep. But she couldn't remember her daddy being with them much. Some said he worked at a lumber sawmill for a time, so he was never home for the noon meal. Since the Simpson men worked the farm, they were there for all meals.

At the supper table they sometimes talked about Lou Ellen as though she was invisible. When she asked for second helpings, or sometimes third helpings of the biscuits and tomato gravy, she'd be the topic of discussion.

"I wonder why she eats so much?" One of the aunts or uncles would ask everybody in general.

"Well, she probably hasn't ever had enough food—maybe she's been hungry a lot." Another would answer.

But the worst of all—was when someone said, "She may have worms." *Now that'd take anybody's appetite!* she thought. Maybe she did have worms! She never got fat. In fact, she was way too skinny because she'd heard them say so. And sometimes at night she dreamed of being devoured inside out by worms—big, long, ravenous ones.

While they were living in the log cabin, Lena's sister, Eva, got married but still lived close. Lou Ellen loved it when Aunt Eva came to visit. She occasionally brought some little trinket or a hair barrette for Lou Ellen. She often combed her hair or just let her sit close to her.

Jeremy was Nathan's good friend who lived close by, and they spent summers together from morning until dark fishing, hiking, swimming in the river, picking berries, and all other normal little boy things. Lou Ellen became their shadow—a genuine tomboy—until they learned how to sneak off without her. Jeremy often ate with them, and the three of them frequently got into plenty of trouble together—especially when they were caught in Granny's pantry eating the flour or sugar.

When Christmas came that year, Aunt Eva decorated Granny's house, complete with cedar tree and homemade decorations. Lou Ellen could hear the adults whispering in another room, but they would shoo her out when she tried to go in. There was something happening and she, Nathan, and Jeremy could sense the excitement in the air. The adults finally told them Sandy Claus—as they called him—was going to bring their presents on Christmas Eve, and they would all get to wait up for him to come. Jeremy and his parents were invited over to celebrate with them and to see Sandy Claus too.

They all gathered in the front room to wait for the mysterious man to deliver their presents, except Aunt Eva, who was in the kitchen cooking. Soon she came to the door.

"Darn it! I need one more cup of sugar to bake my cake for tomorrow's Christmas dinner. I have to run down the road to the Willis house and see if Nelda has an extra cup I can borrow. I'll be right back, 'cause I sure don't want to miss Sandy Claus," she said as she grabbed her coat and left.

The adults laughed and talked, telling jokes and scary tales while the kids ate apples, oranges, Brazil nuts, and sucked on hard ribbon candy. The kids waited impatiently and constantly asked how much longer it would be; but when the knock sounded on the door, they scurried like mice—as far from the door as they could get.

"He's here! Lou Ellen, open the door for Sandy Claus!" Granny said, all excited. But Lou Ellen didn't move. She didn't know who might be lurking outside that door. She just stood there wide-eyed and speechless, shaking her head.

After much coaxing, they were able to persuade Jeremy to let Sandy Claus in. The man standing in the doorway bore no resemblance to anyone Lou Ellen had ever seen, and wasn't anything she had expected either. He was a small, old, funny-looking man with a wide-brimmed felt hat pulled down over his eyes. He wore a pair of dusty, worn-out brown boots that looked like he'd walked a very long way to get to their house. He walked all hunched over with a full burlap sack on his back that Lou Ellen thought might have toys inside, and he carried a rather crooked walking cane that didn't seem to do much to help him take his wobbly steps. As all three kids cowered around the furthermost chair from him, practically sitting on the lap that occupied the chair, Sandy Claus continued toward the tree—where he immediately took a spill into the floor and began to moan.

"Oh! My back! O-w-w! Please...somebody, I hurt my back...*please* rub my back," he said in a weird old man's gruff voice. No child moved.

"Lou Ellen, go rub Sandy Claus's back...go on, he's hurtin'!" her granny said, giving her a little push.

Wild horses couldn't have dragged her one foot closer to that stranger. She would not budge. After much persuasion, Jeremy and Nathan cautiously walked over together and lightly massaged his back. The adults continued to coax Lou Ellen to no avail, until one of them took her by the hand, walked with her, and placed her hand on his back. She reluctantly used one finger to touch him and jerked her hand back as if she'd touched a hot stove. She then ran back to safety!

Sandy Claus's back healed quickly, and he stayed a long time. He ate candy with them and talked to Nathan and Jeremy, who had finally opened up and relaxed a little. Lou Ellen was still too afraid of him to talk, even though he tried to engage her in conversation too.

"Hey! Pretty little girl with the big blue eyes! What's your name?" Lou Ellen hung her head, mute and wary.

"Cat got your tongue, little girl?" he asked. She remained silent.

"I know...I'll bet it's Betsy...you look like a Betsy to me...is that your name?" Sandy Claus asked. Lou Ellen slowly moved her head from side to side, still silent.

"Okay … then it must be Cathy … that's a pretty name … come over here, Cathy, and sit on my lap."

But Lou Ellen wasn't ready to trust the stranger, and she didn't correct him. She didn't want him to call her *anything*. Occasionally she sent a surreptitious glance in his direction, wishing he would leave so she could play with her presents without having to watch her back. In addition to paper dolls, Sandy Claus brought her a much cherished, first and only store-bought doll and some pretty doll clothes. But she still didn't feel comfortable with that strange fellow in the room.

Aunt Eva didn't get home in time to see Sandy Claus, so when she got back the kids talked all over each other—telling her all about him and what had happened—and Lou Ellen was unaware that Aunt Eva and Lena exchanged smug smiles. But Nathan and Jeremy were older and had noticed. Even though Lou Ellen had been terrified of "that man," it was one of her fondest childhood memories. Later, Nathan and Jeremy informed her of Santa Claus's *true* identity that special Christmas. *I worried all that time about Santa's hurt back, and it was Aunt Eva pretending—down in the floor on our level—trying to get us to come closer and relax, be happy, and have fun. At least it worked for Nathan and Jeremy!* she thought.

CHAPTER FIVE

Some of Lou Ellen's memories for the next few years were disjointed and incomplete at best. She later realized that God was in control at all times and had been protecting her. And now, she thanked him and gave him all the praise and glory.

Other than the one spanking over the thrown apple, she couldn't remember getting whippings prior to her new mother's arrival. It was possible, even most likely that she did. But she just couldn't remember any others—probably because she got *so many* thereafter!

Lena was the first person Lou Ellen could ever remember calling "Mother," but as time passed she became convinced her mother hated her. When she asked to do something—*any-thing*—her mother would say, "You'll have to ask ya daddy." Her daddy was at work, never home to ask—so, she just did it! When Daniel came home from work, Lena told him Lou Ellen had done something without her permission, so he'd spank her. It was almost a daily occurrence.

A black cat "took up" at their house that their daddy said was a boy cat, and they named him Blackie-Boy. A short time later they found Blackie-Boy under the house with four kittens! *She* became Blackie-*Girl*. The land where the house sat was sloped, so the front part of the house sat on taller blocks, leaving a high space underneath that was open—not skirted with tin to keep animals out, like some were. Lou Ellen often played under the house, even more often after the kittens were born. She had been forbidden to play with cats, because the adults said they carried diseases. She could sit upright under there to play, and she could see when one of her parents came out of the house to look for her. She'd quickly crawl out the other side before they caught her playing with the kittens. When they called her name, she'd come running from around the other side of the house. They were unaware she'd been just below their legs when they were going down the steps a few minutes earlier.

But one day Lou Ellen got tickled at the kittens pouncing each other and chasing her dress sash, which she'd untied for that reason. Her mother heard her giggling, got up to investigate, and spied her through the cracks in the floor of the room. When her daddy got home, her mother ratted on her ... and he spanked her. *Fun with those kittens was worth all the spankings I got*, she thought.

As time went on, Lena started whipping Lou Ellen herself, and Lou Ellen became an expert at running circles around her to avoid the peach tree switch she used on her legs. She remembered one solitary incident when Lena whipped her with her hand instead of the infamous switch. Both were down on the floor, and with one hand her mother was holding her by the hair of her head as she lay on her back. Squirming away from Lena using her heels, around and around her mother she went, trying to keep her legs out of reach of her mother's other hand. Lou Ellen could never recall what that whipping was for, but she remembered thinking she really hated her mother that day. And she'd never been able to tolerate her hair being yanked since.

At some point—she wasn't sure exactly when—Lou Ellen began to think that either her mother was not capable of making decisions for her because *she* had the mind of a child too; *or* she just *wanted* Lou Ellen to get a whipping. As a small child, she tended to believe the latter. *I must have been a stubborn, head-strong child or I was a slow learner back then, because it seems I didn't learn to make the right choices for myself for several years!* Lou Ellen thought.

Lou Ellen and Nathan antagonized each other and frequently got into arguments and tussles. She'd bite him, and then she'd get a whipping. She was small but feisty and had a quick temper.

Biting was her wisely—or unwisely—chosen method of defense, and it worked. She kept it up! They tried everything to break her of the despicable habit. Several of the adults had bitten her for punishment; they'd even made her brother bite her back. Nothing worked.

Their Grandmother Hudson came to visit while they lived in the little cabin, and Lena told her about Lou Ellen's uncontrollable biting habit. Her grandmother decided that the next time she bit her brother, she would bite Lou Ellen back—and gave her plenty of advance warning. Her grandmother didn't have to wait long, but when she bit Lou Ellen back with her false teeth, Lou Ellen screamed and cried buckets. She'd seen those ugly skeleton teeth in a cup on the dresser—she was scared to death of them! It was so traumatic for her, she sobbed until she got the hiccups. Her grandmother took her on her lap to console her, making her promise that she wouldn't bite Nathan ever again. So they knew they'd found the cure. It worked, but only until the very next time her brother challenged her, and she started biting him all over again! She just could not help herself! They must have given up on breaking her of the habit because her grandmother never bit her back with her false teeth again.

Lou Ellen was fearless... or maybe it could be said that rather than behaving bravely, she behaved rather recklessly at times. She would try anything; therefore, she got "double-dog dared" a lot. Nathan and Jeremy did everything together, and Lou Ellen tagged along, wanted or unwanted, because there were no other little girls around there she could play with. Jeremy often witnessed Lou Ellen's and Nathan's skirmishes, but he never challenged her. In fact, Lou Ellen thought of Jeremy as her brother too—her "good" brother.

A little river snaked through the woods near both their houses, but the adults absolutely forbade any of them to go to the river to swim; they could *fish only*. Jeremy was a year older than Nathan, and the two of them would often sneak off to go skinny-dipping. They always managed to get away without Lou Ellen, so she never learned to swim. Jeremy's mama found out about one swimming trip, and he got into a little trouble. But he'd still sneak off.

One day Lou Ellen went looking for the boys. Down near the water she heard muffled laughter and eased through the bushes to the riverbank. There she found them swinging out on a bamboo vine in a wide arc toward the middle of the deep part of the river and back to the tree from which the vine grew. Sometimes they'd drop from the vine into the middle of the river and swim to the bank. They were having a blast, so Lou Ellen couldn't stand it any longer. She begged to swing too, threatening to tell on them otherwise. So Jeremy showed her how. There was only one problem. He forgot to tell her to stop herself with her foot when she arrived back at the tree. Hitting that tree broadside with a resounding *whop,* she was stunned. She was usually really good at hiding her emotions ... being *tough* ... but she distinctly remembered crying that day.

Quite often in the summer, Nathan and Jeremy took their berry buckets and walked up the winding, woodsy, dirt road, past Nathan and Lou Ellen's log cabin and into the meadow just over the top of the knoll. There they spent hours picking the big luscious, sweet blackberries that Granny Simpson used to make jelly and scrumptious blackberry pies.

One day when they went to pick berries and had their pails almost filled, they suddenly heard the most awful, loud, piercing noise in the edge of the woods nearby. They'd never heard anything like it before in all their treks through the woods or forages of the blackberry patch. They were shocked and frightened.

"W-what was t-that?" asked Nathan.

"I don't k-know," replied Jeremy, "but it sounded like uh…uh…a monster or sump-um!"

Not being the bravest two warriors around, they started to seriously spook. Wide eyed and already practically panting, Nathan whispered, "Oh, Lord, help us…Jeremy…it may be that g-ghost Granny told us 'bout…'member? She said h-he lives in that ol' e-empty Wilson home place…way back y-yonder in them w-woods."

"Nah! That ain't no g-ghost, that's a big b-bear or gorill'er or sump'um. I *know* it is," Jeremy whispered back.

By the *second* time they heard that same noise, Nathan was already in motion, and Jeremy followed suit. They practically knocked each other down as they ran helter-skelter as fast as they could through the briars and brambles of the meadow to the dirt road. Somehow they became separated.

Jeremy looked around to see where Nathan was, and when he didn't see him anywhere, he totally panicked. Running even faster and more erratically, he tripped and spilled his bucket of blackberries, which went flying in all directions down the hill. Quickly jumping up, he kept on running as fast as his feet could carry him to the house, yelling for help at the top of his lungs.

Alarmed, Granny Simpson and Lena ran outside, and Jeremy's mom came running out to meet him. "Jeremy…Jeremy…what's wrong? What is it?" his mom asked, her voice showing deep concern.

Gasping for air and with tears rolling down his face, he gulped, "I…uh…uh…d-don't know, but I t-t-think a…a…m-m-monkey got Nathan!"

In only a matter of seconds, and before the adults had ample time to panic, Nathan came flying around the curve of the road, equally spooked and breathless. Quickly seeing they were both safe and sound, the adults burst out laughing. At the supper table that night everyone had a good belly laugh over that little episode, and the adults just assumed a large pileated woodpecker, coyote, or some other wild animal had spooked the boys. After that experience it seemed Jeremy and Nathan were prone to get frightened quite easily, especially after dark. Perhaps it was the thought of the ghost that lived way back in those woods.

The adults had always loved to tease Jeremy about the time when he was little and had the measles. He was stuck in his house, had to drink sassafras tea, was bored to tears, and feeling sorry for himself. The story they told was that while lying on his bed, he sighed really big, and said, "Ho, ho me, I wekon I'll be dis way a-a-l-l day wong." It was a good thing he didn't know it would actually be *several* "a-a-l-l day wongs."

Lou Ellen had always thought drinking sassafras tea to help accomplish *anything* was just an old wives' tale. Allegedly, it made the measles "break out" more quickly. Who cared? The kids certainly didn't want them to break out quicker! And her thoughts had always been that anyone who'd ever had to drink that vile-tasting stuff understood why the kids thought maybe the adults were just trying to *punish* them.

CHAPTER SIX

When Lou Ellen was five and a half years old, the family moved into a tiny, two-room shanty beside the railroad tracks, two miles from Cloverton. She slept under a window on a cot at one end of the kitchen. The house sat about fifty feet from the tracks, and just a short distance away the tracks then crossed a two-lane highway. To Lou Ellen, it was a terrifying, deafening noise when the train blew its loud warning whistle as it passed their house and approached the crossing. The train was so close that sometimes the little shanty seemed to shake with sheer terror. *Or was it me?* she wondered. But she eventually became accustomed to it, even during the middle of the night. Her daddy, Nathan, and Jeremy had once ridden that train together, but she'd never had a desire to ride it.

There was a big field behind the house where her daddy grew their vegetables, cantaloupes, and watermelons. While he was planting onions one day, she asked him for one to plant herself—one to call her very own. She watched the top grow, but she wanted to see the progress of the rest of it too. So every week or two she dug that onion up, just to see how much the bulb had grown, and then replanted it—much to her daddy's amusement.

Her daddy had a pigpen located a short distance away from the house, where he kept a sow named Sadie. He told Lou Ellen that Sadie was going to find little pigs one day.

"*When* will Sadie find her little pigs?" she asked her daddy almost daily.

"Any day now," was always his same reply.

Daniel got Sadie's food from the school cafeteria, where he worked for a short time as a janitor. When the kids had uneaten food left on their plates, they filed by big metal cans, raked the leftovers into the cans, and her daddy took the "slop" home for Sadie.

After he fed Sadie the slop one day, she got sick. Lying on her side with her eyes closed, she could only grunt—over and over. Lou Ellen was worried.

"Daddy, is Sadie *dyin'?*" she asked.

"No, Sadie's snockered on slop licker, Lou Ellen," he said as he laughed and patted her on the shoulder. "She'll git sobered up when Nathan comes back with the 'mater juice."

She'd been absolutely fascinated by that drunken sow. Her daddy told her the slop always contained sandwich bread, and in warm weather the yeast in the bread caused the slop to ferment if it was left to sit too long. He also told her that tomato juice would sober a drunk man the same way it sobered Sadie. *Maybe so,* she thought, *because Sadie walked around again in no time.*

Then one morning while Lou Ellen was sitting at the breakfast table trying to eat her "pukey ol' sticky oatmeal," her daddy came from the direction of the pigpen, calling her name.

"I'm comin', Daddy," she said, running to the door and thinking how much she hated breakfast food … especially oatmeal.

"Lou Ellen, come quick, come see the little … Sadie's got—" But she was already out the door. She knew what he was going to say; she'd waited for this day too long.

Heart pounding with excitement, she ran down the steps with lightning speed, past her daddy and on to the pigpen. And there was Sadie, lying on her side.

"One … two … three … ," she counted … and counted … until she counted *twelve* little pink piglets lined in a perfect row between Sadie's front feet and her back feet. They were all scrambling and squealing as they looked for breakfast on Sadie's belly.

Sadie had finally found her pigs!

"Ooh, Daddy, *please* go in there and bring one out for me so I can hold it and see it up real close," she said, jumping up and down with anticipation.

"Don't be silly, Lou Ellen. Sadie won't let me mess with 'er *pigs.*"

"*I'll* do it! I'll be quick as lightnin'! I'll grab one and come hand it 'cross the fence to *you* ... she won't even know I was there!" she said as she put her foot on the fence and started climbing.

"Lou Ellen, get down from there! You better *never* go in that pigpen. If you do, *you'll* be Sadie's slop, and I won't have to feed 'er no breakfast, dinner, ner supper. Do you hear me?" Her daddy was nearly yelling.

"Yessir," she said, jumping down with disappointment plainly visible in her face and slumped shoulders.

Lou Ellen was six years old the first time she experienced one of her daddy's "breakdowns." Her memory of the event was sketchy but traumatic, given her young age.

She was standing in the yard with Nathan, Lena, Granny Simpson, and one of Lena's brothers. Her daddy was inside the house, but something strange and scary was going on. Something fearful hung in the air that only the adults knew. She wondered why they were whispering and looking down the road and then back toward the house.

Soon she saw a car coming and watched it as it drove into their yard and stopped. The car had a star on the door. Two men in brown uniforms with stars on their shirts got out, and the adults were talking to them in low voices as they pointed toward the house. Suddenly, she saw her daddy run out the back door and across the garden plot to the lean-to.

"There he goes!" one of the men yelled, as they both ran after him.

The "bad men" went into the lean-to, and in a few minutes they came back with her daddy in front and between them, arms behind his back. They brought him to their car, put him into the back seat, and turned the car around to leave. She and Nathan looked at each other and began to cry. They couldn't understand what was happening.

"Daddy ... Daddy? D-a-d-d-y!" Lou Ellen screamed. As the car pulled away, their daddy turned to look at them through the rear window. He lifted his hands, tied at the wrist with something shiny, and with tears running down his cheeks, he tried to smile as he waved good-bye to them.

She and Nathan stood there sobbing, horrified.

That may have been about the time "the nightmare" started too. But she would think about that later. Sometimes a memory was like being on a journey and approaching a road sign that warned of danger ahead. Her mind usually did a quick u-turn.

The adults sold Daniel's mule and wagon and that sow and her piglets, and the Hudsons went to live on the farm in the house with the Simpson family. Lou Ellen started first grade while they lived there. They walked to school—she, Nathan, and Jeremy. It seemed much longer than four miles each way in winter time than in warmer weather. At school she and her brother were given free food, pencils, and paper because they were so poor. Even at that age, she was aware of being "different" from all the other little girls.

But that was the year of awakening for Lou Ellen. It was the year she learned about a whole new world waiting to be explored and how easy it would be to do. She began to learn to read. Books would become her most prized possessions and her greatest joys in the years to come.

Lou Ellen didn't know how many months their daddy was gone that time; but after he came home, they moved from Granny Simpson's back into their same shanty by the railroad tracks. Somehow her daddy bought or was given another mule and wagon, which they used to travel back to Granny's house to eat dinner every Sunday. It was several miles away, traveling on deeply rutted dirt roads, but she and her brother enjoyed those bumpy wagon trips, especially the two or three weeks while the wild plums were ripe.

"Daddy, Daddy, stop! *See?* Over yonder...see them ripe plums?" Nathan said, pointing.

"Whoa!" Daniel told the mule. "Look out fer snakes now, and don't eat too many worms 'cause they'll give ya a bellyache," he said, teasing Lou Ellen and her brother.

"*Yuck!* Daddy!" Lou Ellen said with disgust, remembering another discussion about possibly having worms. She carefully inspected every plum to make sure it didn't have a worm hole anywhere.

Sometimes her daddy got out of the wagon and picked plums with her and Nathan and took some back to the wagon for her mother. Lou Ellen loved those juicy, sweet plums, but thought she might have enjoyed them even more if he hadn't mentioned the worms. Even so, those had been pleasant memories.

Another one of Lou Ellen's fearless feats occurred while they lived beside the railroad tracks. There was a wide and deep ravine in front of the house, just across on the opposite side of the tracks, which they called the "big gully." The side of the ravine was a treacherous drop, so steep that her daddy had chiseled out the clay sides to make several steps for them to walk up and down.

A natural spring that ran through the center of the ravine was their source of water for the shanty, and they took their clothes there to wash them. Giving the appearance of a small waterfall, the spring poured down from a rocky ledge to a flat sandy area and formed a six-feet-wide basin a couple of feet deep, before flowing on out on more level but still rocky ground. They used buckets to dip water from the basin to tote to the house every day. Once a week they took their dirty clothes to the basin and washed them. Lou Ellen hated helping tote the water because she always seemed to spill most of her bucketful as she carried it back up the steep steps, but she loved the sound of the running water as it trickled over those rocks and fell down into the basin. And she loved the wild violets that grew throughout the rocky crags and crevices even more.

Most of the ravine bank was composed of red clay, but a hundred yards down from their shanty, the bank had veins of chalky white clay woven throughout. She often saw people of color down in that area, digging out the clay—to eat.

One day Jeremy came to visit Nathan, and they played outside in the front yard and up in the chinaberry tree all day. Lou Ellen hung around with them, as usual, and they walked down the ravine and ate *their* share of chalky clay too!

Back in the yard, as it began to get dark, the boys started talking about going inside. But Lou Ellen wasn't ready to go in.

"No-o-o, let's climb the chinaberry tree to the tiptop and look up at the pretty stars," she challenged them.

"I ain't climbin' no tree in the dark," Nathan replied.

"Chicken!" she taunted, hopping up to the first limb to begin climbing.

"She's crazy. She'll try anything," Jeremy said, looking from Lou Ellen to Nathan and shaking his head.

Nathan and Jeremy began whispering to each other, and Lou Ellen's curiosity got the upper hand.

"Tell *me*... tell *me*... I wanna know too," she said, jumping down and coming close.

"Nah, you don't wanna know... you won't *do* it. You ain't that brave!" Nathan said.

"Yes, I will too! Just tell me what it is. Y'all the ones that ain't brave... *bawk, bawk, bawk*," Lou Ellen taunted them, strutting around mimicking the Rhode Island Red rooster at the hen house.

"I bet *you* the chicken... you too chicken to go over to the highway by ya self in the dark," Nathan said, pointing across the big gully.

"Not either!" she said with defiance.

"Well... prove it! I double-dog dare ya."

"Okay, it won't take no time...see ya in a few minutes, you big chicken!" she spat as she started walking.

"Wait! How'll we know you went *all* the way? You might go halfway and turn 'round and come back!" Nathan said.

Jeremy hadn't said much up to now, but he chimed in.

"I know...she can take some matches with 'er and light one up for us to see soon as she gits there."

"Okay...I'll go sneak them matches from outta the kitchen...be right back," Nathan said.

At this point, Lou Ellen started to think about what she'd gotten herself into. She knew the route well. She'd have to cross over the railroad tracks, go down the ravine steps, pass the spring, cross through the overgrown jungle area and climb up the snaky, kudzu infested bank to the highway that led to the next small town...in the dark. She'd never done it in the dark before. On the other hand, she could walk the railroad crossties to the same highway, a much easier and less scary route...and not half as far. But she'd come out at a different spot on the highway, and they'd know she hadn't crossed the ravine.

Seeing her brother returning with the matches, she squared her shoulders and stood tall. *Oh well! Too late now...nobody's gonna call me chicken and get away with it,* she thought. So she set out across the tracks, still too annoyed to think about being scared...until later.

She went down the steps, being careful not to miss one. Just as she approached the area of the spring, she heard a noise she couldn't quite identify. Then she heard it again...a distinct grunting noise, and she instantly froze with one foot in midair! She felt as though someone had poured a bucket of chill bumps on her head, and they oozed over her whole body. She strained to see, but the moon wasn't bright enough yet for her to see what was there lurking in the shadows, waiting to devour her. She didn't know if it was human or animal, and at that point it didn't matter. She knew it *had* to know she was there...it could surely hear her heart drumming and smell her fear.

But it must be some animal that's more interested in water than in a scared dummy, she thought, as she heard it run off through the bushes, down the ravine, in the opposite direction. Her pounding heart gave her energy to move faster and get the trip over with, all the while trying not to think about the snakes in the kudzu. She tried not to think at all! She reached the highway and struck a match, and—just in case they missed it—she struck another. Then she struck her body back across that ravine before her courage burned out like the match flames.

She did it! She showed those silly cowards! But she never told them about how scared she was at the spring. *Maybe I should have… maybe I should have told them about that gigantic black bear and how I scared him off… all by myself!* she thought, as she smiled with mischief.

But then maybe that incident should just be documented as one of her reckless acts too!

Things seemed mostly good when her daddy was home—that is, until his next "sick" cycle. But Lou Ellen always anticipated the good times would come to an abrupt halt any day. When bedtime came she had a great feeling of fear and anxiety, maybe of impending disaster. Was it a fear that the bad men would come for her daddy again? She didn't know. She had always had a bedwetting problem, for which she was always in trouble. She could have been anxious about that, too. And then she began to have "the nightmare" more frequently.

The huge gray blob, looking like a giant balloon, floated into the room, to her bed, stopped, and hovered above her. She was so scared she could hear her pounding heart but nothing else. Then it slowly started to descend… moving at a snail's pace, it crept downward… a little closer… and closer… threatening to crush her. Closer… until it was pressing into her face and nose and she couldn't breathe… suffocating her!

She could almost feel the panic even now.

She was flailing her arms, trying to fight it off, screaming... crying... sweating and gasping for air. Suddenly she was being shaken, someone was calling her name, "Lou Ellen, wake up... wake up... what's wrong?" She awoke to find her daddy hovering over her, and she clung to him, crying with relief.

"My stomach hurts," she'd told him.

She did not know why she never told her daddy about that horrible nightmare. She always responded with the same reply. Sometimes he gave her a dose of baking soda in water to drink. He told her he thought her supper had given her indigestion. She hated the taste, but she preferred to drink it rather than tell him about that dreadful dream. She'd not had the nightmare every night, but much too often.

When she was eight years old and in third grade, the school principal went to Lou Ellen's and Nathan's classrooms and took them out of class. She told them an aunt and uncle had come to see them and that they could go outside to sit in the car and visit with them. When they reached the most beautiful red car Lou Ellen had ever seen, they got into the back seat because there were three people sitting in the front seat—a man in the driver's seat and two women.

"Hello, Nathan and Lou Ellen, my name is Shelly. I'm your aunt. This is my husband, Dennis, and this is my sister, Mary." The woman in the middle said.

Lou Ellen couldn't remember Dennis or Mary turning around or speaking at all. Aunt Shelly had done all the talking. Since Nathan and Lou Ellen were both really shy and reserved, and because those people were total strangers to them, they offered no conversation and responded only when the aunt asked them questions.

"What do you want for Christmas?" was the only thing Lou Ellen could ever remember her asking.

"A bike," she and her brother both told her. And the shiny red car drove away.

When they got home from school that afternoon, Lena met them, asking questions.

"Did somebody come to school to see y'all today?"

"Yes ma'am," they said.

"Did ya know 'um?" she asked, and they both shook their head.

"Well, guess who it wuz?"

"Who?" Lou Ellen asked. She was becoming increasingly curious. *Something strange is going on,* she thought.

"She said they're our kin," Nathan said.

"One of 'um wuz yo *real* mama," Lena said. "They come here too, and they said they'd been to school to see y'all, but ya daddy told 'um to never come back here agin."

"She didn't tell us she was our mama, did she, Nathan?" Lou Ellen looked at him for confirmation, and Nathan shook his head.

"Them people wuz trying to steal y'all and take ya away ... and ya daddy went to the school principal and told 'er never to let that happen agin," Lena said.

Lou Ellen and Nathan stood there speechless. *There go the bikes we asked for,* was all Lou Ellen remembered thinking. She wasn't too concerned about the mama part. She didn't even remember what the lady in the car had looked like anyway.

When their daddy came home that night, he didn't bring the subject up. It was many years before he talked about Mary at all, and he never talked of that incident. To their knowledge, that was the only time Lou Ellen and Nathan had ever been in their biological mother's presence after she left them when they were small.

Since I wasn't aware of it at the time, did it even count? Lou Ellen wondered.

Lou Ellen remembered a humiliating experience she'd had when she was eight years old. Her grade school had a performance night, a variety show for all the parents and townspeople to see. She was given an instrument to play in one of the musical numbers, which was a triangle she struck with a little metal rod when the music leader instructed. She thought that was so much fun, and she was filled with incredible excitement.

At the time, her daddy worked for a man who owned a sawmill. They didn't have a car then, so Lou Ellen could hardly wait for her daddy to get home from work that night and walk with her to school. Time passed and he didn't come. It was getting dark. She approached her mother.

"Mother, please let me walk on to school, and when Daddy comes home, you can tell him to come to school and walk back home with me."

Her mother wouldn't say she could go, but she wouldn't say she couldn't either. So she went! She was on the stage along with the others, playing her triangle when her daddy came in. He took her off the stage in the middle of the musical number, took her straight home, and gave her a spanking.

He'd worked hard all day, walked home, and was much too tired to then walk two miles to the school to get her—his rebellious child. She shouldn't have walked that distance alone after dark either. She understood all those things years later when she had her own children, but at the time, she was mortally humiliated.

When Lou Ellen was nine years old, she and Nathan started school in September and were in the same grade. Nathan had been nearly seven when he started first grade because his sixth birthday came a month after the deadline. He should have been two years ahead of Lou Ellen in school; however, he apparently had problems with his schoolwork and with no one to tutor or encourage him, he failed to pass not one, but *two* grades. Consequently, they both ended up in the same class in fourth grade.

CHAPTER SEVEN

The Hudsons moved again when Lou Ellen was ten years old to another place without electricity or any modern amenities. But this time it was bigger, with four rooms instead of two, and it was only one mile from town and school. She thought it was an unpainted mansion compared to the two-room shanty they had just left behind. It had a long porch extending across the entire front of the house and another porch on the back, spanning the kitchen and dining room. The house was rather run down, with a missing windowpane or two. The front porch was in dire need of repair, and the tin roof leaked in several places.

But things were looking better.

Just six feet from the steps of the back porch they had a well for water, surrounded by a wooden frame, the top of which held a windlass for drawing buckets of water. *Hooray! No more toting water up steep steps from the spring in that ravine,* she'd thought. They had three galvanized washtubs on the end of the porch for washing their clothes—one for washing and two for rinsing.

The tiny kitchen held an old wood stove for cooking and a small rectangular worktable where the wash pan and a bucket of water sat. It had a bottom shelf that held stacked pots and pans, hidden by a skirt made from a plastic tablecloth and attached with tacks to the edges of the tabletop.

Adjacent to the kitchen was a dining room containing a rough-hewn, homemade rectangular dining table with thick legs that appeared to have been carved with a dull knife. Only the legs had been painted white ... a long time ago. A plastic tablecloth adorned with tiny rosebuds was placed over the top to cover the pine knots and rough finish. Sitting on one side of the table were two cane-bottomed chairs, each with one or more sagging broken strips. On the other side there were two wooden slatted chairs, one painted long ago in the same white as the dining table. The other one had been painted different colors over the years, the last being an eyesore brown or eggplant-purple shade, with other equally ugly colors still visible in places. The corner was occupied by a white pie safe with screen doors and appeared to be home-made by the same novice carpenter who crafted the dining table. It held dishes, silverware, and everything else ... except pies.

There was a bedroom with a small chifforobe sitting in one corner, which probably had once been a classy piece of purchased furniture but had long since become someone's redecorating proj-ect discard. The room held two four-poster double beds, which were made of rusty wrought iron and supported sagging dirty mattresses. They sat catty-cornered in opposite corners of the room—one for her brother and one for her. Lou Ellen thought she had died and gone to heaven. She had a real bed—not a cot—and she even had *half* a bedroom!

The fourth room, the "front room" as it was called, was a liv-ing room and bedroom combined. A dark brown sofa, which had seen its best days in some unknown house, occupied the space in front of double windows overlooking the front porch. Another wrought-iron double bed, where her daddy and mother slept, sat in a corner. Beneath the other window was a small rectangular table similar to the one in the kitchen—minus the plastic skirt. An old battery-operated radio with one missing knob sat on top, while the bottom shelf held her daddy's Holy Bible on top of a crocheted doily. A monster-sized homemade wardrobe painted dark mahogany loomed in the corner and monopolized the room. The top two-thirds portion had double doors where her daddy's Sunday clothes hung—donated sports coats, dress pants, and a yellowed white shirt with a frayed collar. Two large draw-ers on the bottom held linens, towels, and homemade patchwork quilts with no rhyme or reason patterns. The wardrobe and the quilts were all donated by relatives, as was most of the rest of the furniture in the house.

A fireplace in the same room made a half-hearted effort to heat it in winter, but her daddy complained that most of the heat went up its chimney. Perched above the fireplace was a mantle, blackened on the bottom from years of soot and ashes that had drifted up from countless fires. It held her daddy's brown alarm clock, which he had ordered from the Sears and Roebuck catalog. She thought it was a drab thing, but she had to admit it was a perfect compliment for that nasty mantle. Every night he would wind that clock, a grating sound that seemed to go on forever and that grew to increasingly annoy Lou Ellen. It signaled time to blow out the lamp and get to bed, and it always seemed to be right when she was in the middle of the best part of her book. *I hated that clock,* she thought.

All the windows in the house were bare except for two in the front room. They had plastic rollup shades, one of which had a broken spring and didn't work. None of the other rooms were heated except the kitchen, which was heated by the cook stove, but only when meals were cooked. Later on Daniel either bought or someone gave him a small black wood-burning stove, which he placed in the front room. Compared to the fireplace, it worked much better to ward off the frigid winter air that seeped through the cracks in the walls and floor. Occasionally her daddy could afford to buy coal to burn in the stove; but not often enough.

Not long after they moved there, Lena got pregnant. Lou Ellen remembered her being sick and throwing up a lot. But in the third month, she lost the baby, and she never slept in the same bed with Daniel again. She slept in the double bed with Lou Ellen until she got married and moved away. *So much for half a bedroom of my own!* she thought.

Other than the one special, unforgettable Christmas at Granny Simpson's house, the Hudsons didn't celebrate Christmas. They didn't decorate, had no tree, no special meal, and no presents. It was just another day. It was the same for birthdays. She and her brother grew up just knowing that was the way it was at their house. She thought that decorating and buying presents were probably a mother's responsibilities, but her mother took no initiative, child that she was ... or *wanted* to be. Lou Ellen thought they just didn't have money for those kinds of things; however, when he did have the money, their daddy always bought apples, oranges, fruitcake, nuts, and hard candy around that time of year. The scent of orange peels burning in the fireplace was one of her fond memories.

But that first Christmas in their new house was different. Their church brought a bag of gifts on Christmas Eve and left it on the porch. At least, her daddy thought it was from their church, but they were never sure. Inside, in addition to fruits and candies and some practical items, was a beautiful bride and groom doll in a small white box with a cellophane front, so you could see them through the box. Since she was the child, Lou Ellen knew it was meant to be hers, but her mother took it, set it on the mantel, and forbade her to take the dolls out of the box. She actually coveted those bride and groom dolls. A couple of years later, occasionally she had been allowed to get the box down and set it on the couch to play with, but she still could not remove them from the box.

CHAPTER EIGHT

Lou Ellen never knew why her daddy only went to school a short time in the seventh grade before dropping out. His Papa, as he called his daddy, may have taken him out to help on the farm, or it could have been because of his mental health. She was never told. In any case, he'd always worked a lot of different jobs over the years. He was a hard worker and seemed to be good with math.

In the summertime her daddy mowed lawns to make money. Often he didn't collect any money because if it was a widow lady who he thought didn't have much, he only charged her a couple of dollars—or nothing at all. That was especially true when she brought him out a plate of food for lunch. He then told her that the delicious, best-he-had-ever-eaten food was pay enough. Oftentimes some of it had been food he had furnished himself, because he gathered some of all the vegetables he grew and delivered them to many people around town. Many times Lou Ellen had heard her daddy say that the Bible said the men of the church should always take care of all the widow ladies.

Other times after her daddy finished whatever job he had done for them, some people would tell him they would pay him later, but often they never did. More than a few times she heard him say, "That's okay. They probably needed it for something else more important."

One of Daniel's occupations was that of a well digger. He dug *new* wells for people whose wells had dried up; or he just dug their existing wells deeper, when they wanted. He would also clean out wells that needed it. Sometimes an animal, chicken, or snake would fall into a well and die. The water would start to stink, and the owner would hire her daddy to clean it out. It was not a job for anyone who was claustrophobic, and it was extremely hard and dangerous work. However, if or when they paid him, it was decent wages. When he dug a new well, he charged by the depth, so each amount varied. Though they always seemed to have food of some kind to eat, there was never money for clothes.

People gave the Hudsons bags of hand-me-down clothing, some good, some in need of repair, but all greatly needed and appreciated. Her mother, who was very thin, got first choice of the girly things; then Lou Ellen could have the rest. The chifforobe in their bedroom had four small drawers on one side and a hanging section with a mirror on the other side that held her mother's dresses. Lou Ellen's dresses and skirts hung on nails on the walls because there weren't any clothes closets in the house. Sometimes in summer "dirt dobber" wasps entered through the screenless open windows and doors and built mud nests in the folds of her skirts and dresses. She remembered too many frustrating occasions when she got dressed for school and then had to quickly change because she found a mud nest filled with wasp eggs in her skirt.

When Lou Ellen was eleven years old, Aunt Eva made her a dress of soft, yellow satin-type material and crocheted a darker yellow L at intervals all around the bottom of the skirt. She loved that dress. When she'd been in first and second grade, Aunt Eva had made her some flour sack dresses from material in which large sacks of flour were purchased. Sometimes some of the girls at school made fun of her dresses because they usually had large flowers and were loud colors. So the yellow dress was like a princess dress to her—her prized possession.

Lou Ellen had become independent at a young age. She had taken over her own laundry chores at ten years of age because her mother made her wear her dresses two consecutive days before she could put them in the laundry to be washed. She hated it when one of the other girls commented, "You wore that yesterday." So she washed and ironed her own clothes and could wear what she wanted, when she wanted. What she wanted was to be as unnoticeable as possible—to blend into the crowd.

While ironing her clothes one day, Lou Ellen started to press the cherished yellow dress with one of the heavy irons that had to be heated on the stove or in front of the fireplace, and which had no method of adjustment to control the heat. She placed an iron that was far too hot to the lower skirt section of the dress and promptly melted the material. Feeling totally devastated, she sat down on the floor and cried. Maybe her mother felt sorry for her that day because she told Aunt Eva, who took the dress and patched the skirt; but it was just never the same. *Like I sometimes felt, it was marred, damaged, and scarred—imperfect!* she thought.

On freezing cold nights of winter, those same irons sometimes served a dual purpose. Heated in front of the fire in the fireplace, then wrapped in a blanket, they were ideal to put under the covers at the foot of the bed to quickly warm cold feet when they first went to bed. Lou Ellen had additional means of keeping *her* feet warm. She always had a yard cat or two—strays who wandered in and stayed—even though she was forbidden to handle them. That was one of the rules she had bent a lot.

Her bedroom had a window with a missing pane when they moved there, but they couldn't afford to put a new one in. Her daddy had put cardboard in the window, but from rain and sun it had worn out, leaving one corner loose. In the winter, her cat, Simon, would sneak in through that cardboard, jump into her bed, and nudge her face until she lifted the covers and let him go down to the bottom to sleep at her feet. They kept each other's feet warm.

The door between her room and the front room where her daddy slept made a scraping noise when opened. After her mother told her daddy the cat was sleeping in bed with Lou Ellen—and therefore her mother's bed too—her daddy would come in and try to catch the cat in bed. Simon got wise. The minute he heard the scraping sound, he bounded out of her bed and was out the window in a flash. Her daddy was seldom even close to successful. She always rooted for Simon and silently cheered when he won!

Simon was Lou Ellen's best friend and companion, and he got an ear-full all the time, especially when she was mad or upset about something and just needed to vent. She had created an imaginary playhouse out under the pecan trees. It was just an old wooden platform, the floor portion of a room that had once been in the old run-down, partially collapsed building across the road from them, which her daddy brought to their yard for some reason. Lou Ellen pretended Simon was her husband, and she cooked many fine "gourmet meals" fit for a king, just for him. He ate every one of those delicacies she put in front of him, including tomato and potato peelings she took from the garbage! He must have been really hungry because they didn't buy food for the animals. Feeding the humans had been challenge enough. Cats and dogs ate leftovers, when there were any, or they used their innate abilities and caught their own food.

Lou Ellen and Simon spent a lot of time out there in the playhouse because he was a great listener! But one day, Simon was nowhere to be found. A few days later he re-appeared, but he had a wound, which the adults told her, or she presumed, was from a cat fight. There was never any money to take a pet to the veterinarian; so she watched him get sicker and sicker. When he died, she was utterly devastated. She felt that everything she loved had a habit of eventually disappearing. She didn't go near that playhouse again for weeks.

That was also around the time she created her imaginary friend, Abby, to talk to. In those days, in her house at least, children were to be seen but not heard. They were definitely not allowed to have opinions or defend themselves, not even against each other—at least not in hearing range of the adults. The understood but unspoken word was *quiet!*

In summers when there was no school, Lou Ellen had limited interaction with other people since they didn't live right in town. She wasn't allowed to go to town alone except for the week when Bible school was in session. She didn't know where Nathan was during those summers, unless he was away helping their daddy in the gardens, or playing with Jeremy, whose parents had moved to town by then. Since he was three years older, he could go and do things she couldn't do, whether he was supposed to or not! Consequently, she had not had a human being she could talk with, most of the time.

Then one day Lou Ellen became so bored and lonely she went out to play in her playhouse under the pecan trees again. She draped her long-sleeve flannel shirt on the back of a discarded, old dilapidated, cane-bottom chair she had confiscated from the trash for her playhouse, and she pretended it was her best friend, Abby.

They had a lot in common. Lou Ellen pretended Abby was an orphan whose own mother and daddy had just abandoned her in the middle of an old country dirt road one day when she was two years old and never came back for her. She was taken to the orphanage, where she lived a lonely existence, except for the hot summer afternoons when she would sneak out of the orphanage to spend time with Lou Ellen in the playhouse.

Abby was taller than Lou Ellen, but they were both too thin. She had bright green eyes; long, naturally curly, auburn hair; and a sprinkle of tiny brown freckles across her perky, little, tipped-up nose. Lou Ellen thought she was exceptionally pretty and sweet, and they talked endlessly.

"What do you want to be when you grow up, Abby?" she'd ask.

"Oh, I think … maybe … a nurse!" Abby said. And they had discussed what little they knew about the nursing profession—the blood, the guts … and the screaming.

Lou Ellen asked Abby the same question again in one of their subsequent play sessions, but this time her answer was different.

"I just want to be a pretty little girl with a real mommy and daddy who love me and will never leave me," she said. "And I want to have plenty to eat and wear."

After their screaming scenes discussion, Abby didn't want the nursing career any more. *Or maybe it was the blood and guts,* Lou Ellen thought.

"How about you, Lou Ellen, what would you like to be?" Abby asked.

"I just want to marry a good, handsome man who will love me ... I want to live in a pretty white house," she said, with a faraway dreamy look. "And I want to have babies to love, lots of clothes, food, and good friends I can invite over to see me."

Noticing the hurt look in Abby's face as she turned away, Lou Ellen wanted to reassure her.

"Abby, you will always be my *bestest* friend. Nobody can ever replace you, and you can live in my house with me forever. I promise," she said. Lou Ellen felt fortunate that she had one parent who provided for her when he wasn't sick. At least she had a house to live in, even if it was practically falling down around her.

On a few occasions, Lou Ellen told Abby exactly who she wished she had for a mother. The name changed frequently and was generally always an adult woman who had recently been nice to her, or just talked to her ... anyone who seemed the least bit interested in her, and hopefully could even learn to love her.

Lou Ellen and Abby passed many giggly, gabby, happy hours together out in that imaginary home under those pecan trees. Abby helped to keep her spirits alive and sufficed for the human companionship she craved. But those pleasant times couldn't last forever either.

CHAPTER NINE

When Lou Ellen and Nathan started seventh grade, their mysterious aunt and uncle tried to visit them at school again, but the principal prohibited it. They never knew whether their biological mother was in the car with them that time or not. Perhaps they no longer cared. Eventually, Lou Ellen convinced herself she had *never* cared.

It was during the seventh grade that Nathan finally gave up trying in school, dropped out, and got a job pumping gas and doing odds and ends at a service station. But it was the beginning of even more troublesome years for her brother.

The Christmas Lou Ellen was twelve, she made a brave effort to decorate. She went into the woods and cut the top half out of a cedar tree, took it home, and propped it in the corner. She spent hours making homemade paper decorations for it, but when she finished decorating … it just wasn't *quite* right. It needed lights. After giving it some thought, she came up with what she thought was a bright idea. On her way home from school the next day, she stopped in town and bought a box of birthday candles and Scotch tape with her meager savings. When she got home she taped the candles all over the tree, and just as she was opening the box of matches to light the candles, Jeremy came to visit.

"Jeremy, you're just in time! I'm so glad you are here … come see … I just finished my masterpiece," she said as she ran out to meet him. "I was just about to light it up!"

Taking him by the arm, she positioned him just where she wanted him, opened the matchbox, and lit all those candles.

"Abracadabra!" she said, stepping back and stretching out her arms toward the beautiful tree. They had about ten seconds to admire it before those cedar limbs and paper decorations burst into flame and Jeremy had to help her smother the fire! As a child, that was her one and only attempt to decorate a tree, because to her, lights *made* the tree. Without lights it was just a green tree.

When her friends at school asked her every year what she got for Christmas, Lou Ellen made stuff up. She sometimes named some of the used clothing they had been given months before. She knew they were not like everybody else, and she desperately wanted not to be different. But she did *not* want their pity! She was glad her birthday always came during the summer, so she didn't have to fabricate a cake and all the birthday gifts she hadn't received.

Year by year, Lou Ellen became more aware of just how totally different the Hudson family was. She never asked her school friends to go home with her. She was embarrassed. They sometimes invited her to their house, which was how she learned to compare. Oh, how she wanted to live in a painted white house, have electric lights instead of a kerosene lamp, and a bathtub or shower instead of a porcelain wash pan. And an indoor toilet! Like her friends from school. She just felt so ... all wrong—like her wrong name, wrong mother, wrong house.

Because he was so strict, people said Lou Ellen's daddy was a religious fanatic. She was not allowed to wear shorts, make-up, lipstick, nail polish, go to the movies, wear a swimsuit, or go to the swimming pool. She couldn't read comic books or play cards, and she definitely could not dance nor read those "trashy love story" magazines and books. She couldn't participate in extracurricular school activities such as attending football games, and she was not allowed to participate on gym night, since it required her to wear shorts. Even her friends at church could do most of those things, except they were not allowed to read those trashy love stories either. That was the only taboo thing she sort of understood at that time. She had once told someone that if it was *fun*, it was forbidden at her house.

Lou Ellen wanted so much to just be a part of gym night at school. She broke another rule and borrowed some shorts during Physical Education, went through all the routines, practiced, and pretended. For a little while she belonged ... she was a part of something. She enjoyed it right up to the big day, secretly knowing she would never be allowed to attend the night of the actual event.

CHAPTER TEN

When Lou Ellen's daddy was home and mentally okay, he was a little less strict, and he could sometimes be fun to be around too. He was a laid-back practical joker who loved to cook and eat too. He was officially the cook of the house, and he experimented a lot. Besides homemade biscuits and regular everyday food, he sometimes cooked great doughnuts, cracklin' bread, and blackberry cobblers. He made pure blackberry jelly and prided himself on never using that "Sure Jell junk that messes with the flavor." His expertise included awesome homemade ice cream and soft peanut candy made with cane syrup. All cooking was done on a wood stove he insisted was the *only* kind to cook on.

In summer her daddy grew plenty of fresh vegetables when he was well enough. He had gardens in various locations. People who didn't use their own garden plots or had some fallow land would let him use it to grow his vegetables … and theirs too. He often took Lou Ellen with him to work in one of the garden plots and taught her how to put soda to corn, dig the new potatoes and sweet potatoes, and pick peas, butterbeans, and green beans. There were plenty of different gardening chores—some she liked and some she hated.

One year a neighbor let her daddy milk one of his cows "on halves," which meant her daddy got half the milk and the neighbor got the other half. Her daddy taught her to milk the cow too. Even though she didn't particularly like some of the chores, she loved just spending the time with him. She was secretly very afraid of that cow, especially when Bessie stopped eating, turned her head around, and looked at her with those big brown eyes while Lou Ellen was sitting on the stool by her back leg milking her. And she hated it when Bessie kicked over the bucket of milk or hit her in the face with that long tail tangled with burrs. *Anger probably made me a better milkmaid, though, because milking a cow had not been easy work for small hands,* she thought.

Sometimes her daddy raised chickens, and he ordered the baby chicks from a catalog, which were shipped through the post office. It had amazed Lou Ellen when she went with him to the post office to pick up those cheeping little yellow balls of down. She couldn't understand how they survived all that way in those cardboard boxes with holes in the sides for air—but no food or water.

Quite often Daniel took Nathan and Lou Ellen fishing in the summer. They mostly ate chicken and fish for meat, *when* they had meat. The majority of the winter months, they had meatless meals, and beef was extremely rare at their house any time. Occasionally their daddy killed a rabbit or a squirrel, which he fried and then simmered in gravy and made "lighter than air" biscuits, as he called them. It was delicious to hungry kids.

One morning Daniel didn't have any flour left to make biscuits for breakfast, so he made "egg bread" using cornmeal, eggs, and buttermilk. When that crusty, hot bread came out of the oven, he buttered it and poured syrup over it. From that day on Lou Ellen and Nathan often begged him to make that delicious egg bread for breakfast, instead of biscuits.

Lou Ellen could only remember one occasion when her daddy was home long enough to raise a pig big enough to slaughter and process. Her mother's family and some neighbors and other people came to help with the hog killin' and to share the meat, as was the custom in those days. He had a smokehouse where he cured some of the meat, and she watched them making country sausage to smoke in it too. They had fresh pork for many weeks after that day, but the one pork dish her daddy never cooked was the well-known—though not necessarily widely loved—dish that some Southerners called "fried chitlins." He gave those parts of the pig to someone who *did* love them.

Lena had always said Lou Ellen's daddy could cook better than she could. She didn't have much experience. Lena just didn't cook! There had been one exception to that general rule. She was known for cooking great collard greens, the best Lou Ellen had ever eaten anywhere. Her mother just didn't *like* to cook. So she didn't if Lou Ellen's daddy was home to do it. She had never even wanted to make the decision of what choice of food to cook. Later on when Lou Ellen was older, her daddy had assigned the supper cooking chores to her if he had a job and knew he wouldn't be home in time to cook.

Cooking supper in the wintertime was no big deal because in the cold months, when there were no fresh vegetables other than a variety of greens, supper was almost always just a boiled pot of one thing, such as dried lima beans, dried black-eyed peas, turnip greens, collard or mustard greens. And there was always corn pone bread baked in the oven. Most of the time their only meat in winter was a ham hock or small piece of salt pork cooked in with the dried beans, peas, or greens, just for seasoning. Although she remembered often being cold, Lou Ellen couldn't remember ever going to bed hungry as a child; but their meals were certainly not considered well-balanced meals during the cold winter months.

When their supper meal was a pot of greens, they sometimes had sweet potatoes baked in the oven at the same time as the corn pone—if her daddy had been home to grow, harvest, and store them.

Storing the sweet potatoes through the winter was unique to Lou Ellen. Her daddy dug a hole in the ground near the house about the size of two washtubs. He lined it with layers of pine straw, put the sweet potatoes in, packed more pine straw over them, and covered it with burlap sacks. Then he used tin or wood planks to stand around it in the shape of a short tee-pee, to shed water away from the bed. It had designated areas to be used to take the potatoes out as they were needed, and afterward the opening had to be properly re-covered.

She absolutely detested hearing her daddy say, "Lou Ellen, go dig sweet taters for supper." She was terrified of putting her hand down into that potato bed. She was certain it also harbored rats, or worse yet, a bed of rattlesnakes!

She'd once had a bad experience down at the henhouse when he sent her to gather eggs. As she reached into the open end of one of the old apple crates used for nests for the laying hens, something made a noise and moved. Thinking it was the hen still in the nest, she dropped to her knees and leaned close to get a better look at eye level.

The eyes looking back at her caused her to gasp for breath and fall back! Her arms and legs felt like rubber, her backbone tingled, and her skin was covered in prickly cold pimples. She couldn't move or speak. Her head started to spin, and she thought she was going to pass out. She'd passed out once when she cut her foot with her daddy's axe; she knew the signs.

But she quickly recovered enough to let out a blood-curdling scream, which immediately brought her daddy running. She scrambled a safe distance from the apple crate, tears streaming down her face. Instead of a hen in the nest, her daddy dragged out a long rat snake that had just swallowed the egg. She was *not* fearless that day, and she learned to check out the occupant of the nest first and foremost in the future!

Nor was she fearless the day her daddy dragged home a large rattlesnake for Lena and her to see. It was six feet long, and the middle of its body was six inches in diameter. It had been in the process of swallowing a rabbit when he found it. Even *dead* that snake was terrifying! She didn't know whether he had killed it or the half-swallowed rabbit was the cause of its demise, but she never forgot the size of that rattlesnake or the bottom half of that poor rabbit hanging from its jaws. To her, a snake was deadly to humans no matter what species it was. A green garden snake, a king snake, or a rat snake was just as deadly as a rattlesnake. Either one could evoke a heart attack!

When they didn't have money to buy plenty of kerosene for the oil lamp, Lou Ellen had to get her homework done before dark.

In the winter months they mostly always went to bed shortly after dark for just that purpose—to avoid burning so much kerosene. The practice was two-fold because it saved the wood they burned in the fireplace or heater as well. In cold weather she sat by the wood stove in the kitchen and did her homework as she cooked supper after school, but there was rarely any extra daylight for her favorite hobby, reading. Consequently Lou Ellen had dearly loved spring and early summer because the days were longer, and she had plenty of daylight to do her homework before school let out for the summer ... and then to read.

During all her childhood, when her daddy was home and well enough, he made sure they went to church every time the doors opened. He didn't *send* them; he *took* them. But Lena never went. She was uncomfortable in crowds and would have attacks of what she called "my nerves," so she wouldn't go anywhere, except to her mother's. Anything she refused to do was because she "wasn't able," and since it wasn't an illness she could define, she just said it was her nerves. When people asked how she was, she always responded, "I believe I feel *some* better." Lou Ellen often wondered when she would be "*all* better" or "all *well*." "Sick" to her mother meant attention, and her daddy supplied. He often fetched her drinks of water while she sat in the rocker and rocked! In later years someone asked Lou Ellen how long her mother had been in such bad shape, and she told them her mother had been dying for at least twenty-five years! They thought she was joking!

School usually started every September, immediately after Labor Day. When he was home, their daddy took Lou Ellen and Nathan to pick cotton during the month of August and on Saturdays in September. Since Lou Ellen goofed off a lot with all the other kids in the cotton field, she was not too productive. Her daddy just added what her sack of cotton weighed to his total, and the farmer paid him for all of it. But her daddy always gave her some money, and she saved it to buy used school textbooks after she entered high school.

While picking cotton was definitely *not* their choice, Lou Ellen and Nathan managed to have fun playing with the other kids in the wagons full of cotton—burying each other or standing high on the sides of the wagon to dive into those fluffy soft beds, over and over. Then best of all were the memories of raiding the watermelon patch nearby! The melons were hot, and their hands certainly fell far short of sanitary, but nothing ever tasted better—not to mention the fun they had in the seed-spitting contests.

Around age twelve, Lou Ellen became aware that her mother was probably mentally challenged—merely a child living in a woman's body, without the ability or desire to make decisions. Or in retrospect, Lou Ellen thought perhaps that was how she wanted to be perceived because it meant she would have no obligations or responsibilities. In either case, Lou Ellen had become more and more the adult of the house, and her mother was the little girl. Lou Ellen felt that ultimately she had raised herself, since for one reason or another her daddy was not home much. At times during certain stages of his illness, for many weeks he would be there physically while being absent and totally unaware mentally.

Grandmother Hudson visited them every year and always stayed a month. She darned all the hand-me-down clothes and put patches on the holes of Daniel's and Nathan's worn overalls. She re-hemmed Lou Ellen's dresses or skirts that had hems unraveling, and she taught Lou Ellen how to crochet. She gave them some much-needed attention that one month a year. She loved to fish and could sit down by the river, or even just a puddle-sized brim pond, and fish all day long. Lou Ellen loved her grandmother and sat right there and fished with her a lot, but she may have talked more.

Daniel loved his Mama, as he called her, and all his big family of seven half brothers and sisters and seven of his own brothers and sisters, a grand total of fifteen young'uns. His mama lived to be eighty-seven years of age. *Grandmother Hudson, you deserve a medal*, Lou Ellen thought.

Lou Ellen never heard her daddy distinguish between his whole siblings and his half brothers and sisters, who were from his daddy's first marriage and whose mother had died; he seemed to love them all equally. Her daddy was the youngest son, so half of the older ones were married and moved out by the time he was born; but he had a good rapport with all of them. Family gatherings were important to their large family.

Many of her daddy's family were musically talented, and they all loved to get together and play musical instruments and sing. Some of Lou Ellen's most pleasant memories were of going with her daddy and Nathan to her Grandmother Hudson's annual birthday "dinner on the grounds." It was always held in the fall on Sunday afternoon at the family's "little old country church," where their granddaddy Hudson was buried, about fifty miles away. They had not always been able to attend because her daddy was sometimes ill then; but when they did go, they went on Saturday and usually stayed overnight with one of her daddy's brothers or sisters who still lived in that area. They had lots of cousins to play with, since they usually stayed with their uncle and aunt who had twelve children of their own. *They probably didn't even notice when three more people showed up for supper and a bed!* she thought.

After the feast was over the next day, they all gathered around the piano inside the church and played and sang. One of their aunts played the piano, one played the organ, one uncle played guitar, and her daddy blew a harmonica. The rest just sang! Sometimes even the kids would wander in and sing a little. Lou Ellen remembered singing "Peas in the Valley," which she thought were the words of the often-sung old-time favorite gospel song, "Peace in the Valley." In those days they usually had to travel by bus to the birthday dinner, and it seemed Lou Ellen almost always got motion sickness. It was still a fond memory of hers.

CHAPTER ELEVEN

The first signs that indicated Daniel was starting to get "sick" were irritability, sleeplessness, agitation, hyperactivity, incessant talking, and incomplete thought processing. All those signs foretold that bad news was imminent—it was only a matter of time.

One moment her daddy could be laughing hysterically, and the next, crying as though someone had merely flipped a switch. Irrational thinking caused him to do odd things at even odder hours, such as going to someone's house at midnight and waking them up for something insignificant, saying the ox was in the ditch, and it couldn't wait until morning. He often started a conversation about one subject, but before he finished it, he'd start another, then another.

In a matter of weeks, he became unable to sit down long enough to eat, lost weight to the point of being emaciated, and had severe headaches and hallucinations. Finally he became fearful and listened for helicopters overhead coming to bomb them. He seldom shaved, got his hair cut, or took a bath. He kept a light burning and stayed up all night until daylight, fearfully watching for whomever his confused mind conjured up. If or when he slept, he catnapped during the daylight hours. During those times he was anti-doctor, anti-medicine, and denied he had a problem at all. While in those early stages of bizarre behavior, Lou Ellen didn't even recognize the man he was becoming. He wasn't the same man she called Daddy.

One of the stages he went through was an obsession about reading the Bible, and he read it all night and into the early morning. There were times he would wake Lou Ellen and Nathan up in those wee hours and make them sit on the couch and read the Bible out loud until they couldn't keep their eyes open and kept collapsing in sleep. Each phase of his illness lasted weeks, sometimes months.

Without intervention, he eventually went into severe depression and became catatonic, never leaving his bed unless absolutely necessary. At that point he was compliant. He ate when food was prepared and set before him, but he didn't speak unless spoken to. He seemed to be unaware of conversations going on around him. She thought if they'd had proper medication to give him, he probably would have improved without incarceration at that point. But in those days, the usual procedure was to take him to an institution for help.

Most of the time *before* Daniel progressed to that amenable stage and accepted help, he was such a nuisance to family, neighbors, and others around town that someone was forced to get help for him. By that time, Lou Ellen, too, was ready for them to come for him because she knew then he would get better.

People often speculated about Lou Ellen's daddy's illness. Many said the Bible drove him crazy... periodically. Some said he might have a brain tumor. Others said it had to be cyclic because he started getting sick every spring when the sap came in. The speculations and opinions were endless. Lou Ellen paid close attention, and she noticed that her daddy's illness did not start every spring, as they said. And what they called "periodically" turned out to be every year or eighteen months—not always in the same seasons. She often wondered if *she* read the Bible too much, would she get sick too? She had no one whom she trusted enough to talk about it, but the thought was always in the back of her mind.

When Lou Ellen's brother was a teenager, he started to rebel. He had been working at the service station and other jobs around town for about a year when he started staying out later, smoking, drinking, and disobeying his daddy. Like her, there wasn't anything he was allowed to do that was fun, so he rebelled. She had her books for pleasure, but Nathan didn't like to read. When Daniel was sick, he was extremely tough on Nathan. He would wait up until the wee hours of the morning for him to come home, and then whip him with his belt, saying, "The Bible says to spare the rod is to spoil the child."

As time went by, Nathan asked Lou Ellen to help him out by unlatching the door leading from the front porch to their bedroom before she went to sleep; and she did...as often as she remembered. When he came home late, he could quietly sneak in and get into his bed. In the morning when his daddy asked what time he got home, Nathan never told him the true time. For a while, it worked.

One night Lou Ellen forgot to unlatch the door. While Nathan was trying to wake her by calling her from the window, Daniel heard him, and her brother's punishment was one of the saddest childhood memories Lou Ellen had. She purposely pushed it away and refused to think about it for many years, because it brought tears to her eyes and a sad, heavy heart. She didn't know how often the exact same thing happened, or if there was ever more than one time. One was all she could bear to think about, even now.

In an early hour of that chilly morning, Daniel tied Nathan to the clothesline post, beat him with his belt, and then drew cold water from the well and poured it over him. Lou Ellen woke up and listened to his screams piercing the quiet night, too afraid to interfere because their daddy was at a terrible stage of his illness then. She was a coward. She knew it was all *her* fault for forgetting to unlatch the door! The stab of guilt and the pain in her heart was almost palpable. She should have at least tried to help him, to beg her daddy to stop. Instead, she put her head under the covers, put the pillow over her head, and curled around her own pain. She was nearly thirteen years old, but on that painful night, she reverted back to a three-year-old child and remembered the words that had comforted her then.

"Jesus wuvs me, dis I know, for de Bible tells me so. Wittle ones to him bewong. Dey are weak, but he is strong." She hummed the words over and over in her head, until she cried herself to sleep.

Her brother would always carry the physical and emotional scars from that beating, and she would always carry a scar in her own heart...and guilt. She locked that horrible memory away in the deepest recess of her brain and refused to recall it. She wanted it erased because it was an anchor in her boatload of sad memories—one that was too heavy and threatened to sink her.

Lou Ellen never understood why Nathan wouldn't mind their daddy. Why wouldn't he come home on time, do what he was told, go to bed, then get up and leave in the morning for work? She had always preferred *no* attention over *negative* attention. But later she learned it was a common teenager rebellion stage Nathan went through. His home life just compounded the problem, and without a mentor, he chose the wrong path. Things only got much worse for him for years, even after he ran away from home. He got involved with a circle of friends where crime was a common choice of career. His friends were older, wilder, and street wise. They often flirted with disaster and death. Though Nathan had a gunshot wound scar as a reminder of that time in his life, by the grace of God he survived until he found his own way.

Most often, help for Daniel in those tumultuous years of Lou Ellen's childhood usually meant involuntary admittance to a mental institution so they could give him medication. After he was put on medication for a few months, he was on the road to recovery for a year or maybe a few months longer, if they were lucky. But getting help for someone who resisted with everything in his power was traumatic, for him as well as for all others involved. It usually meant law officers with handcuffs, after he hid in the pantry or barn with his shotgun. He said the gun was for his own protection, not to kill anyone with, because the Bible plainly said that killing was a sin. Of course those officers didn't *know* he wouldn't turn the gun on them or himself. However, her daddy was well-liked around town, and no one wanted it to end tragically.

Lou Ellen understood even then that they had to be careful when dealing with someone as sick as her daddy was, but the authorities could always talk him into giving up and coming out in the end. Even so, it made her sick with fear that he would shoot himself or be shot by one of the officers. To make the situation even sadder was the fact he was always taken to jail to wait for a couple of days, or however long it took the judge to get the paperwork processed to admit him to the institution. Those were all extremely sorrowful experiences that she could only have endured through God's love, comfort, and protection, and she was thankful.

CHAPTER TWELVE

In the throes of summer, in a house with no electricity and consequently no fans, the Heart of Dixie sunshine seemed to drain the life from every living creature: human, animal, *and* pest. Even the flies lit somewhere and sat there dazed, but not for long enough. At Lou Ellen's house all the windows and doors were left open to catch any hint of a breeze that might chance to pass by. Without screen doors and with no screens on the windows, the flies in the daytime and mosquitoes at night were a relentless, terrible plague. Her daddy tried everything he knew—or could afford—to repel the mosquitoes, but nothing worked consistently. One method he often used fascinated Lou Ellen. He took a metal bucket and started a fire in the bottom. He then took a rag and pressed into and around it just enough to put out the flames; but it still smoldered. Smoke wafted throughout the room and settled on everything. There was surely more finesse to it than that, but that was all she could remember. Purportedly the smoke repelled mosquitoes. Lou Ellen could never decide which was worse … the acrid smoke that made her cough or the mosquitoes that made welts and sores on her arms and legs.

Even her new cat, Tom-Tom, wouldn't come inside when the smoke was so strong. He was a stray that wandered in one day, and Lou Ellen secretly fed him. Tom-Tom had a strange meow that her mother detested, but he was Lou Ellen's new friend. She thought he was the most beautiful color, like a big juicy orange.

Because of the mosquitoes, flies and other pests, it was a miracle they never had malaria or a lot more illnesses than they had. Although she had numerous bouts of sore throat, tonsillitis, and common colds, Lou Ellen could only remember one occasion when she thought she was seriously ill. She had a fever and sore throat, and large swollen nodules appeared in her armpits and neck. She had no energy and just wanted to sleep. Her mother repeatedly said Tom-Tom had given her some rare disease, but the local doctor told her daddy it was "glandular fever" and gave her some medicine in capsule form. She'd always had a big problem taking pills of any kind, even small ones, and as horrible as castor oil was to take, she would have chosen it over a pill any day. After she was finally able to swallow those horse capsules, she sometimes ended up throwing up some of them, and then her daddy worried she wasn't keeping enough of the medicine down to get well. In later life, she read that her illness was just another name for mononucleosis, and bed rest and fluids were all that was recommended. *Horse pills for nothing,* she thought.

Lou Ellen was brought up in church and had Jesus in her heart. She prayed to him, and she knew from a small child that he was always there for her. But she was also terribly afraid that, like people said about her daddy, maybe too much Bible and religion could drive a person crazy. When she was almost fourteen years old, she publicly professed Jesus as her savior and was baptized, but she was still afraid to completely commit that tiny little piece of self-control to him. She didn't want to go crazy, do weird stuff, and go to an institution. But she knew without a doubt that God loved her. Without him, she couldn't have survived emotionally during some of her worst experiences.

There was a tiny closet in their front room, which had shelves for storage and was probably meant for linens. It hadn't been cleaned or organized for years and was overflowing with rags, old clothes, papers, and other junk. One day Lou Ellen chose to clean it out, organize it, and then take the pile of junk to the pasture to burn. Her mother sat and watched her clean and then walked with her to the pasture.

She wasn't sure how it happened, but somehow some of her daddy's bullets or shotgun shells, or a combination thereof, was in the junk…maybe in a pocket or a box of papers. The hot fire soon ignited the bullets, which started exploding one after another, then two and three at a time. Scared out of their wits, both she and her mother ran like the wind. It wasn't the Fourth of July, but they'd had some real fireworks just the same—albeit unintended, perilous, and scary ones. Even though she was almost fourteen years old, she came dangerously close to getting a whipping from her daddy for that incident…and for wasting his ammunition.

From the time she was small, Lou Ellen's mother's family had always been the ones to get help for her daddy when he became ill, since her mother assumed no responsibilities. When Lou Ellen was fourteen years old, the Simpsons decided *she* was old enough to do it herself. By that time Nathan had run away from home and was living in another state. They told her she had to go to the judge and get papers signed to commit her daddy. She dreaded it so much that she was actually physically ill. Just the word *judge* scared her. She wanted to coward out, but it was not an option. Her uncle drove her to the courthouse in Pikeville to sign the papers, and they told her they would send someone to pick her daddy up to transport him the following morning.

Her daddy had been sick so long he was in the deep depression stage. He didn't converse, couldn't focus on any of his responsibilities, or care for the animals. He just sat, zombie-fashion, staring into space with a blank expression, doing whatever he was told, and speaking only if spoken to several times. When she got home, she approached him.

"Daddy?" Lou Ellen said in a gentle voice. He didn't respond, seeming not to have heard her.

"Daddy, can you hear me? I need to talk to you." She spoke louder and put her hand on his shoulder.

He sighed and looked up at her, his eyes vacant, as though he had been in another place and time.

"Daddy, you need help. Will you go to the institution if I ask somebody to take you?" she asked, holding her breath, hoping her mother hadn't told him she'd already made the arrangements.

"Yeah, I'll go back up yonder if you want me to," he said as he hung his head and went back to wherever he had been.

Relief flooded over Lou Ellen. She was so thankful she didn't have the fearful part to go through, but she loved him and felt compassion for him. While his other stages were more traumatic and trying for her and everyone else, it was even more heart wrenching for her to see him in this severely depressed stage.

Early the following morning she sat beside him, dreading the moment when they would come for him. He *said* he would go voluntarily, but she was still apprehensive. *Would the sight of the law enforcement vehicle evoke a bad memory? Would he react to it and change his mind?*

Soon two deputies drove into their yard to take him to the mental hospital, several hours away. She walked out to their car and asked permission to ride with them because she didn't want him to go alone, and they agreed. She was the one responsible for sending him, and she was filled with guilt and sadness ... and dread because she'd never been to an institution before and had no idea what to expect. Going back inside, she approached him.

"They're here for us, Daddy. Come with me ... I'll ride with you."

Her daddy did not respond, except to obediently walk with her and get into the back seat, and she got in with him. Neither of the deputies, nor her daddy, spoke to her during the entire trip.

When they entered the hospital, two staff members met them and led her daddy to an area with two gigantic heavy metal doors, and she walked beside him.

"This is as far as you are allowed to go," one of the orderlies said to Lou Ellen.

When they unlocked and opened the doors to take him in, she could see patients inside and was jolted by the obvious mental condition of several patients—some sitting, a few just standing around, and one chanting some unintelligible words.

"Wait...let me say good-bye to him," she said.

She hugged his unresponsive body, told him she loved him, said good-bye...and felt as though someone was squeezing her heart in a vise. Her daddy stood there with his back to her as the heavy doors closed behind him with a loud metallic clang. It was an almost unbearable sight and sound, yet they were recorded in her mind and preserved forever. Back in the car, with a bruised and aching heart, she turned her face to the window and cried silently, trying to prove she was strong. And again, neither of the deputies spoke a word to her on the return trip.

No one was home when they dropped her off, not even Tom-Tom. The empty house echoed the hollowness in her heart; she'd never felt so sad or alone. Drowning in doubts and fears, she just wanted to go back in time and be three years old again. Once again she wanted to curl in a corner somewhere, fetal-fashion, and sing her favorite childhood song, "Jesus wuvs me."

She was teetering on the edge of despair. She had just locked away the one person who mattered most to her. Now, she was the one locked away in her own self-made prison...unloved and unwanted, on her own.

The only sound Lou Ellen heard in the room was the ticking of the alarm clock on the soot-blackened mantle. Normally unaware of the routine sound, now its slow cadence beat a hypnotizing rhythm in her head, steadily increasing in volume and tempo with each tick until it merged with her pounding heartbeat and threatened to become a raging thunderstorm.

As a storm of emotions assaulted her, her legs failed to support her, and she collapsed to the floor in a painful eddy of turmoil. Rivers of tears ran down her face, splitting into tributaries that dripped from the eave of her chin, raining on her blouse. She sat there sobbing until she was drained of all energy and will—a mud puddle of nothingness. Finally, she melted onto the floor in slow motion as all feeling deserted her too, and she finally found her escape in sleep.

Lou Ellen awoke with a start and for a moment was disoriented. She had no idea how long she'd slept, or for that matter what time she'd gotten home. But she did know she was hungry. She made her way to the kitchen, then to the pie safe in the dining room, but she couldn't find anything to eat. Knowing her mother would be at Granny's, she decided to go there. She washed her face in a pan of water, patted it dry with a towel, combed her hair, and sat down to think ... to think about what she needed to take with her.

Thinking was a mistake. Doubts and fears came creeping back to taunt her, *"It's just you ... you don't have anybody now ... you're on your own ... alone!"* She started to shake. Despair again threatened her senses like a silent thief. With a racing heart, she bowed her head and did the only thing she knew to do. She prayed. "Please, God, help me!"

Suddenly she sensed a presence, a warm, comforting presence, as though it was close enough to hold her ... and then ... it *was* holding her. She felt safe and calmer. From somewhere deep within, a still, small voice spoke to her.

"Lou Ellen, you are never all alone; I'm right here holding you!"

She raised her head listening intently, basking in the comfort and warmth she felt, and little by little she began to calm down even more ... and then to *feel*. Her numbed brain began to function again ... to reason. It was true she was physically alone. She *could* give in to despair and fear of the unknown, like losing one's way in the inky darkness of a moonless night. Instead she prayed again. She didn't know *what* to pray; she just prayed. And she knew that God heard her because she began to gain inner strength and hope. She was able to slowly fan to life that tiny spark of her spirit that was still burning somewhere deep inside her.

She would not cave in. She was a survivor! Her joy, strength, courage, and spirit were severely squashed, but not destroyed. She picked herself up to move on, with hope for better days to come.

Lou Ellen and her mother moved back to Granny Simpson's house, which by then was in town too. Her gramps had passed away, and one unmarried son, Scott, still lived with Granny. He had a good job, had bought them a house, and moved them from the country to town. Built in 1900, it was a colonial-style home painted white with all the amenities, though outdated. Single lightbulbs at the end of long cords hung suspended from an unbelievably high ceiling in the center of each room. It didn't have central heat and air; some of the rooms were not heated at all, while others had small propane gas space heaters.

A front porch with huge white columns extended across the entire front of the house and served as a favorite spot of entertainment for her mother and Granny. Every afternoon they sat in the white rockers or in the swing, which was suspended on chains from the ceiling, and watched people drive by. They knew almost everyone who passed by the automobile they drove. They'd be sitting there every afternoon when she walked home from school. She'd get her homework up while she sat out there with them and listened to them talk.

"Looka yonder…Mr. Brown's goin' back to town again. That's twice now…I wonder where he goes to when he goes up there so much," Granny would say.

"Ain't no tellin.' Oh, there goes Martha Faye! It's Fridy. She gits her hair done on Fridy," Lena would answer.

"No, Martha Faye gits her hair done on Saturdy so it will be purty for Sundy. She must be goin' somewhere else today."

Lou Ellen was glad she had lessons to get up and then a good book to read. She thought that would bore her out of her mind to just sit there and watch cars go by.

After Daniel was taken to the institution, his car, mule, chickens, and pigs were sold—as they usually were when he had to go away. Not long before he'd gotten sick, her daddy had bought the car and had a job going door-to-door selling spices, flavorings, and other products. His car had been full of those products, all of which they'd had to return to the company. Lou Ellen was so sad for him then, but later she understood. She was sure they had needed the money, and there was no one to take responsibility for caring for the animals anyway.

Uncle Scott was good to Lou Ellen and her mother. Sometime during the month of December, for the past two years, he had given both her mother and her a little money around Christmastime, and Lou Ellen had usually bought a pair of new shoes, which she always badly needed. Since she walked up and down that gravel hill, over a mile each way to school every day, they wore out much too soon. Even the best made shoes she owned, such as the popular black and white oxfords, failed to last long enough.

She remembered the last time her Uncle Scott had given them their Christmas money, and she'd stopped in town to buy her new shoes. All the girls were wearing little black ballerina type slippers, and she simply could not wait to get hers. Unfortunately, the store didn't have her exact size, but she wanted them so badly that she bought a pair anyway, a half size too small. Ultimately, she lived to sorely regret that decision. Those soft-soled shoes nearly killed her as she walked that gravel road every day, and she was not sad when *that* pair quickly wore out!

Lou Ellen and her mother lived at Granny Simpson's only a short while that time before moving back to the house under the gravel hill. Her daddy had recovered quickly since he was more cooperative when he was in the deep depression stage and was more receptive to medicines. Or so she'd thought! That wasn't what had *really* taken place "back up yonder."

CHAPTER THIRTEEN

When Lou Ellen was home, she did as she was told and didn't lie. Well … maybe a little *white* one now and then, as she liked to think of them. But she thought of it more as just not telling all or telling nothing at all. That was another area where she and her brother had differed greatly. Their daddy had always drilled into them that if they lied to him when he asked them a question, he would spank them. She remembered that once when she'd been six years old and he was at work, she and her brother went into the watermelon patch and cut open several melons before they finally found a ripe one. When their daddy discovered the melons, he confronted them each separately. Lou Ellen fessed up right away, but her brother lied; therefore, he was punished and she was not. It always made her mother mad when he got a spanking and she did not. She always felt it was because her mother just wanted her to get a whipping too.

Lou Ellen knew in her heart she was far from perfect. When she was away from home, she sometimes gave in to peer pressure and did things she knew were wrong according to her daddy's rules. On several occasions, she tried cigarettes with the girls after school, but she didn't like those at all. She never did figure out how nearly coughing oneself to death on that stinking smoke could be considered fun. But it *was* fun to do what the other girls were doing … just to be one of them.

She borrowed a swimsuit one day and went swimming with a school group in a city pool in another town. It was a Physical Education planned trip on the school bus, and she loved it. She played hooky from a few school classes now and then and went home with a girl from her class who lived in town. They just hung out together, but honestly, she thought it was kind of boring to have nothing to do. Reading a good book was a lot more fun.

One day after school, Lou Ellen and several other kids went to someone's private lake to swim. She couldn't swim and didn't have a swimsuit, but she went along with the group to watch. They enticed her to *wade,* so she took off her shoes and was walking into the water when she suddenly had a horrible pain in the side of her foot. She got out of the water and saw her foot was dripping blood, and she could feel herself start to pass out. She quickly sat down as the other kids gathered around. One of them told her she'd stepped on a broken jug someone had thrown into the lake. They wrapped the wound, put her on a bike with one of them, and took her to the doctor in town for stitches and a tetanus shot.

Dr. Baxter was also the pianist on Sundays at her church, so Lou Ellen told him the truth when he asked how it happened. Next, her only problem was what she could tell her mother and daddy. She knew she would be in trouble either way, but going to a lake would be the worst of all troubles. She wasn't totally truthful with them. To get a lighter punishment, she told them she took her shoes off to wade in a puddle that had a broken bottle in it. *Well, it really was! A very big puddle!* She rationalized.

Lou Ellen always heard people around town saying nice things about Dr. Baxter. They said he had a good heart and always took care of everyone who came to him, regardless of their ability to pay. But she knew her daddy and mother were sticklers about debts they owed. They always paid them, no matter how long it took—a few dollars at a time. So she'd added a burden, which made her feel guilty—her real punishment.

A rather unpleasant incident occurred when Lou Ellen and two other girls were riding on one bicycle. They were taking her home from a GA meeting that had been held at the church after school. The girl "driving" lost control of the bike while going down the gravel hill to her house, and they were thrown into the ditch. Lou Ellen was knocked out, so one girl ran on down the hill to get Lou Ellen's mother, who always freaked out when the least little thing happened. Lou Ellen could not remember anything about the fall itself. As she became fully conscious, she was aware of great pain in her shoulder and neck, and she was walking on tiptoe down that rocky road to her house, supported on one side by her mother and on the other by one of the girls. Each step was torture.

Since her mother was a basket case, the other girls made the decision to go back to town and get someone with a car to take her to Dr. Baxter. She had a broken collarbone, and since it couldn't be put in a cast, she had to wear an arm sling for weeks. The worst part about that incident was that she had been forbidden to ride a bike. She knew the whipping was next; however, by some miracle, she'd only been chastised. She felt that her daddy must've decided her injury was punishment enough. It was.

Lou Ellen learned early, from experience, that obeying was the best way to stay out of trouble, be ignored, and left alone. Whatever her daddy said, she mostly tried to abide by, with only an occasional exception. Consequently, her mother called her "Daddy's little girl" in her mocking, derisive voice and constantly looked for ways to belittle her, telling her she was ugly and hateful. It was much like bully sibling rivalry, except her mother was the adult, supposedly, and Lou Ellen was not allowed to talk back to her. She definitely was not allowed to bite her mother, but there were plenty of times she wished she could have bitten her until she bled!

She kept everything inside. It was an indefensible situation. Criticism was the only thing on the conversation menu at her house—all prepared just for her—but *she* could not participate. She lived with it constantly, and she often felt she just *existed* there. She grew up painfully shy and sensitive, lacking any iota of self-confidence and convinced of her ugliness. Sometimes she felt like her emotions melted into ugly little mud puddles in her brain. She began to live just one day at a time, retreating into her own shell with an invisible wall surrounding her to protect her feelings. As long as she kept that barrier up, she could not be hurt. It was a desolate, cold, and lonely existence. No one ever told her they loved her or gave her hugs and kisses ... not even her beloved grandmother when she came to visit once a year. She loved, but no one assured her that they loved *her*. *I'm just unlovable,* she'd thought.

She didn't consider herself a daydreamer. She did not sit around and dream about being rich and famous one day. Other than the dream to live in a painted white house with all the amenities, the only other dream Lou Ellen had as a child was to one day have her own clothes, ones no one else had worn first, like the cherished dress her Aunt Eva had made her, but with shoes to match! And as she got older, she dreamed of one day having a loving husband and children.

By the time Lou Ellen was a freshman, her imaginary Abby was coming to visit her less and less often, until one day she stopped coming at all. Lou Ellen dove into her schoolwork and activities, her novels, and other escapes, which resulted in no extra time for imaginary stuff. Besides, she now had another *real* best friend, her cat, Tom-Tom. She closed the make believe chapter of her life. Abby had fulfilled her purpose.

Lou Ellen was growing up.

CHAPTER FOURTEEN

During high school, Lou Ellen had mentors who encouraged her and gave her emotional and monetary help as well as glimmers of hope. Miss Watson was a retired teacher who was her Sunday school teacher at church. The summer between Lou Ellen's freshman and sophomore year, Miss Watson fell down the steep wooden steps on her back porch, breaking her leg. She hired Lou Ellen to go to her house twice a day, help her with meals and laundry, and walk to the post office in town to get her mail. Lou Ellen made $5 a week, which she saved to buy used school textbooks that September.

She loved her job because Miss Watson took time to actually *talk* with her. In one of their many conversations, Miss Watson asked her if she had thought about what type of career she was interested in after high school.

"Miss Watson, I know it can't ever happen because we don't have *any* money, but I wish I could go to college and be a nurse when I graduate."

"If medicine is your interest, then you should pursue it," she said.

"I've been practicing for *years*. When my mother has a headache, I put a cold cloth on her head, and I massage her temples," she said. "I think I'd like to help really sick people feel better...maybe I could even make them well."

"You most certainly can go to college, even if you *are* poor; you can get a job and you can work your way through college. You just set your goal and never, ever give up...just go for it, Lou Ellen!"

She never forgot Miss Watson's emphatic reply. Their conversations were always positive and encouraging to her. It didn't happen overnight, but day by day she gained just a tad of hope and confidence in herself. Gradually she began to find little nuggets of faith and determination buried under the layers of self-doubt and fears that had been created by years of criticism and rejection.

Miss Watson didn't live long enough to know that Lou Ellen did not pass the test. She'd passed out at the sight of blood—not only as a child, but also as an adult—so nursing was out! How she wished she could tell Miss Watson what'd really happened later.

Granny Simpson had a neighbor whose husband passed away, and since she was afraid to stay alone at night, she asked Lou Ellen to stay with her. She couldn't remember earning money for that job. What she did remember was taking those wonderful hot tub baths and sleeping in the softest, sweet-smelling, big bed! She wasn't sure if she would have woken up, even if a band of robbers and a posse had shown up! As a bonus, she was sleeping, however temporarily, in a painted white house!

The fall Lou Ellen was fifteen years old and was a sophomore, her daddy bought a battery for the old radio on the table in the front room and switched the one knob back and forth to control the volume, tune, or change the dial. They listened to the Grand Ole Opry on Saturday nights, but when he was working during the day, Lou Ellen tuned in to the nearest station with good reception. It was a country music station that played a lot of Hank Williams, a popular singer who was a native of Alabama but had died a few years before. After his death, he became even more famous and had three top of the chart hits the year after he died. The DJ also played music by Eddie Arnold, Carl Smith, and many more country artists. But the one she remembered best was an artist they just called Elvis. They didn't·play him often enough, but she loved it when the plaintive strains of "Love Me Tender" came across the waves. It stirred a pocket in her heart she didn't know was there, a pocket of longing, but she wasn't sure why.

Jeremy graduated from high school that year and married one of his classmates, Sue Olson. Even after Nathan left home, Lou Ellen and Jeremy had remained good friends ... more like brother and sister. Sue quickly became Lou Ellen's dear friend too. That fall Jeremy found a job in a city an hour away, so he had to stay in the city during the week and come home on weekends. He and Sue had an apartment in town, not far from Lou Ellen's house. Sue was afraid to stay alone at night, so she asked Lou Ellen to stay with her.

Since Sue was four years older, Lou Ellen valued her opinions, and Sue became one of her cherished mentors. Sue taught her a lot about manners, cooking, cleaning, clothes, and makeup; and they remained friends throughout the years. Jeremy and Sue were always there for her when she needed help. Lou Ellen would never forget that. But too soon, they moved away.

When Sue moved, Lou Ellen became an even more avid reader. She lived through her books—no, *escaped* through them. She sailed the oceans blue, soared like the eagles, and vacationed in English manors and the Scottish highlands and many other exotic locations. She'd even gone on safari to Africa once. She had a life no one knew about, a life she enjoyed beyond measure.

To be exact, she had a *lot* of "escapes." She joined everything there was to offer at school or church that involved after school hours in order to stay away from home as long as possible. She excelled in school because when she did go home, she did her homework first. But she was never without a book through which she could elude everything unpleasant.

Her mother even ridiculed her for reading all the time, telling others, "She's always got her nose stuck in some ol' book."

Her daddy didn't censor her books, and she thought he must have felt they were okay since they were from the school library. She didn't tell him about the great romantic love stories in the classic novels in the library, such as *Wuthering Heights* and *Jane Eyre* and so many more.

As she got older, her daddy was a little less strict when his mental health was good. When she was in her sophomore year of school, she had a tube of lipstick, and although he didn't forbid it, he made fun of her when she put it on to go to school. She solved that. She waited until she was well on her way to school every morning before she applied it.

Lena gave her the silent treatment a lot as she got older because she became more and more jealous that Lou Ellen was going places and doing things she, herself, couldn't do. Those times when Lou Ellen attended an event or church meeting after school, her mother would be pouting when she got home and wouldn't talk to her; she wouldn't even acknowledge her presence. When Lou Ellen had a date, she received the same treatment when she got home. If her mother was already in bed when she came in from a date, then she saved her pouting punishment and jealousy until the next morning.

Many times before Lou Ellen went home in the afternoons, if she'd earned and saved any money, she used some to stop in town on her way home and buy a candy bar she knew her mother liked, hoping she would be in a better mood and be nicer to her—sweeten her up so to speak. Sometimes it worked, sometimes not. Finally, deciding that silence was far better than criticism or rejection, she quit trying so hard to please her. Instead, she went home and buried herself in a good book, where a world of unimaginable dreams awaited her.

Miss Daniels was Lou Ellen's Home Economics teacher who taught her to cook and sew *and* took her under her wing. When Miss Daniels made trips to the larger towns nearby, she bought fabric remnants and gave them to Lou Ellen to sew herself some school clothes. Sometimes she suggested Lou Ellen could sew in the classroom after school hours while Miss Daniels graded papers or whatever she needed to do.

As she was leaving class one Friday, Miss Daniels said to her, "Since I have to come into the classroom tomorrow to do some things, would you like to come with me and use one of the sewing machines while I am here?"

"Oh! Yes, ma'am. I surely would," she said. She was so excited. She sometimes sewed on Granny's old pedal machine, but the electric ones in her classroom beat the heck out of pedaling.

"All right, then. I'll pick you up at your house tomorrow, right after lunch. See you then."

Miss Daniels just sat and read a book that Saturday while she sewed. It hadn't been hard for Lou Ellen to figure out that it was out of kindness Miss Daniels chose to use her Saturday to help someone less fortunate...and repeated the scene many times thereafter. Sometimes Miss Daniels discussed and recommended a book she was reading, which she either loaned Lou Ellen or could be checked out from the library. With no small amount of gratitude, Lou Ellen always remembered that teacher's generosity and kindness.

The pharmacy in town, called the drug store, was owned by a man and woman known to everyone, even children, as just Jack and Joan. They were active in the church where Lou Ellen was a member. Joan played the organ on Sundays and played the piano for choir practice. They did not have any children of their own, but every school year they sponsored a couple of students in band, students whose parents could not afford to buy or rent musical instruments for their children to join the band.

During her sophomore and junior years in high school, Lou Ellen had been blessed to be the recipient of Jack and Joan's kindness and generosity. She didn't ask to be, and she never knew why they chose her. They asked Lou Ellen if she wanted to be in the school band, and they paid the fees for renting the instrument she played, the cornet. She would always be grateful to them for giving her the awesome opportunity to learn music. Somehow Lou Ellen was able to scrape the money together to buy the white shirt and long white pants the band members were required to wear while performing and marching.

Although she still lived inside her protective shell at home, she began to gain just a grain of self-assurance away from home. But most of the shyness and lack of confidence were still there, hidden underneath a layer of thin ice, which sometimes came across as unfriendly to others. She told herself that someday she'd come out of that shell. She'd say what she thought; she'd express her deepest feelings. Nobody would tell her what she could or couldn't do; she'd do what she wanted. Someday she'd fly away. She'd be a free spirit.

Someday ... she made a big mistake.

CHAPTER FIFTEEN

When Lou Ellen started her junior year of high school, Amy was a girl in her class whom she liked a lot and buddied around with at school. Amy was a couple of years older than Lou Ellen, but she had failed to pass a grade or two; consequently, they were in the same class. Lou Ellen spent the night with her one night and got to know her mother, Merlene. She thought Miss Merlene was witty and a lot of fun to be around. Amy's house was not painted white either; her toilet was an outhouse too, and her lights were supplied by oil lamps just like Lou Ellen's.

That night Miss Merlene told them that if they would eat salty boiled eggs at bedtime and not drink any water—just go to bed really thirsty—they would dream about who they were going to marry. Amy had a boyfriend, and she wanted to know if he was "the one." Lou Ellen just wanted her future Romeo to be revealed. Amy's mother boiled the eggs, and with much excitement they followed directions. But it just wasn't meant to be. Amy got sick and threw up her salty boiled eggs even before she finished eating them, and Lou Ellen never dreamed anything! *So much for old wives' tales,* she thought.

Amy often took a picture to school of her boyfriend, who was several years older than her. She also took pictures of her first cousin, and she talked about him a lot. Lou Ellen thought he was so cute, but she didn't tell Amy that she was interested because he was a year older than Amy, three years older than Lou Ellen—*too* old, she knew. He had already graduated high school in another town, and Amy told her he had just come home from serving six months of active duty in a military reserve capacity. Besides, she had never even met him in person. She thought he probably was not nearly as cute as his senior class picture anyway. Then one day not long after school started, Amy dropped out of school, got married, and moved to another town. Lou Ellen missed her terribly. A few months later, she heard Amy was expecting a baby.

Dee was another friend in her class who lived in Juno, a town close by that was too small to have a high school. She was bused in to Lou Ellen's high school until she was old enough to drive her daddy's car, and sometimes Lou Ellen was allowed to do things with her. Dee had been going steady with her boyfriend for a year or more already, but Lou Ellen was not dating anyone at the time. As a matter of fact, she had not been really serious about any boy and had not dated many at all. Her daddy was so particular about when and where she went, most boys were not interested in even asking.

The following spring after Amy's baby was born, Lou Ellen asked Dee to take her to visit Amy and to see the baby. During the trip, as usual, the subject of boys came up.

"Amy has a cousin who goes to my church. He's not dating anyone ... think you might be interested?" Dee asked.

"Oh! He's sooo cute. Amy showed me his pictures. If he wasn't so *old*, I would date him in a heartbeat!"

"He's not that old, Lou Ellen! Besides he's real nice, goes to church—"

"My daddy would have a hissy fit. He'd never let me go anywhere with a boy that old, probably not even to church!" Lou Ellen said.

The conversation turned to other subjects, and Lou Ellen forgot about it.

Not many teens had summer jobs when Lou Ellen was growing up, unless their daddy owned a business and they had to help out. One day the owner of the local restaurant, Miss Dixie, saw Lou Ellen passing the café and stopped her to ask if she was interested in a couple of hours of work every week. Lou Ellen said she needed a little spending money and agreed to help her out.

Immediately after church on Sundays, she worked as a waitress at Dixie Belle's Café, Cloverton's only restaurant, where a lot of the locals gathered after church. She didn't make enough money to brag about, but she ate a delicious meal, which was part of her pay...the *best* part.

During her junior year, Lou Ellen was voted by her classmates to be the junior class candidate for homecoming queen. In those days at her school, the queen was not selected by popular vote. Instead, the candidate who donated or earned the most money for the school was the winner. Some of the candidates had bake sales, car washes, asked businesses for donations, and did everything else they could to earn money. Lou Ellen worked hard, but the senior class candidate won the crown. Since Lou Ellen didn't have the money to buy a gown or shoes for homecoming night, she borrowed them. The only problem was that the color of the gown was turquoise, and the shoes were bright avocado green! Luckily the queen's court just sat on the floor of the flatbed truck, around the queen, as the float circled the football field. The spectators couldn't see anyone's shoes. *That experience may have contributed to my later shoe fetish,* she thought.

At home, nobody ever said anything about her good grades on her report card, so Lou Ellen became her own best critic. Good was not good enough to her. She became an overachiever. She had to do better than everybody else because no one else expected anything of her—a nobody. By the time she was a junior, her class consisted of a mere twenty-five students, but only one student, Sheila, had grades higher than Lou Ellen. Sheila had always been a straight-A student since grammar school, the real brainy type.

Lou Ellen's high school was comprised of grades seven through twelve. There wasn't a junior high or middle school—just a "low school" or "grade school" which was located in another part of town where students attended grades one through six. Lou Ellen was chosen from her eleventh grade class, along with one student each from the remaining five grades and asked to participate in a trial subject called "speed reading." The principal and teachers were evaluating the prospect of having the class as a viable, worthwhile learning tool to be offered as a subject in the future. Lou Ellen was carrying a maximum of subjects already, but it was a short trial period, only a half-hour class, and she thought it was fun.

In addition to be being active with the school band, she tried out for a role in the junior class play and got the part. She discovered acting would be easy to do. She could talk and act as somebody else easily enough, just not as herself. She was thoroughly enjoying memorizing her part while her life seemed to accelerate into the fast lane of busy. She was no longer bored.

Toward the end of her junior year, Miss Walden, her homeroom teacher, called Lou Ellen aside after class one afternoon.

"I just want to tell you that I am proud of you, Lou Ellen. Your grades are good . . . the second highest in this class, and if you continue as you are and keep up your current grade point average during your senior year, you could be the salutatorian at your graduation ceremony."

Probably any other student would have been elated to hear that, Lou Ellen thought. But it literally terrified her! She could not, would not get up to speak in front of anybody, not to mention an assembly! She would have absolutely no voice whatsoever. She would rather not have a diploma!

When she was sixteen and a half, and only two and a half months before completing her junior year of high school, Lou Ellen's life took a distinctly different direction. In the span of a few short moments one afternoon, her life changed drastically and dramatically.

PART TWO

BOUNTIFUL LOVE

CHAPTER SIXTEEN

The pleasant smell of coffee penetrated the deep recesses of her sleepy mind at the same time she sensed his presence.

"Good morning, beautiful!"

Lou Ellen struggled in her limbo of slumber for a few seconds before awakening fully to see Burt standing by the bed. He held a cup of steaming hot coffee that smelled of hazelnut cream— her favorite morning scent. Slowly stretching, she yawned and smiled at him.

"How are you this morning, honey?" Burt said, caressing her cheek. "I didn't want to wake you, but you've always told me to never let you sleep past seven a.m. because you feel like you've wasted too much precious time when you sleep longer."

"*Seven?* Is it seven o'clock... *really?*" she said, jumping up, putting on her housecoat, and opening the drapes to bright sunlight. Normally she would've already been up for an hour.

"It's seven oh five, to be exact. Did you have another night of insomnia?" Burt asked, putting her coffee on the night stand and then turning on her favorite morning news program.

"No... not really... at least not once I finally got sleepy. I wasn't in the mood to read, so I spent some time on the veranda again, listening to the pleasant sounds of all the night critters."

"I didn't hear you get up. I vaguely remember you coming back to bed at some point, but I was too groggy to even look at the clock."

"I think I came back inside around two a.m., so I guess I got my *usual* five hours of sleep."

Noticing that Burt's attention was drawn to a news update about the ongoing war, she walked into the bathroom. After she'd brushed her teeth, she made her way toward her recliner in the sitting area of the bedroom to wake up with her coffee and the news. With a wide yawn, she leaned against Burt, who was standing in front of the television.

"I just don't know how you can operate on five hours of shut-eye every night, honey. I need at least seven, preferably eight," Burt said, reaching for her and wrapping his arms around her with one of his affectionate bear hugs. She put her arms around his waist and snuggled in, basking in the love and protection she always felt when he held her.

"I guess I'm just one of those people who doesn't need a lot of sleep. I'm glad you woke me up. I made some plans yesterday with Cecily."

"Oh? What do you two have up your sleeve this time?" he asked, gently massaging her back and shoulders.

"Nothing that's *fun,* I assure you! She's coming to help me clean inside windows today … and probably tomorrow too. There are too many windows to do in one day."

"Oh! No! Don't even look for me. I'll be flying below the radar! I don't do windows!"

"So just *why* do you think I asked Cecily instead of *you?* Don't you think I know you pretty well by now?" she teased while trailing feathery little kisses across his face.

"Okay, Miss Smarty Pants! What am I thinking right now?"

"How many guesses do I get? Never mind … I only need *one—*"

"Wrong! I was thinking about how very much I *love* you! Gotcha!"

"Oh! What a sneaky man you are!" she said, laughing. "You *know* I can't argue with you on that subject."

"What time did you say Cecily is coming?" he whispered, tenderly kissing her lips and ending the discussion.

"I didn't," she whispered back.

"Do I need to put a "Do Not Disturb" sign on the door?"

"Probably not; she's not coming until nine o'clock."

"Perfect!" he said, moving to close the drapes and turn off the television as Lou Ellen turned on their favorite radio station that played soft, romantic music.

Prompt as always, Cecily arrived at nine. Lou Ellen had already gathered all their window cleaning supplies, and they wasted no time starting their chore.

"Do you want me to start in another room, Miz Lou?"

"No, Cee, let's work one room at a time together, so we can catch up on our talking. We haven't taken time to do that in a long while. I've been meaning to ask how your daughter, Lawanda, is doing. Last time we talked, she and her husband were having troubles."

"Aw...Miz Lou, they just don't make good men like me and you got no more. That man of Lawanda's...well...it's like his *brain* just gets scrambled sometimes, and he does crazy things...like buyin' stuff they can't afford and puttin' them in debt. But she loves him. Says she made a vow and she's gonna stand by it."

"Is she still going to church?"

"Yes'um. Lawanda's a good girl. She's got more faith than two folks. She says it's what keeps her goin' sometimes. But I still worry 'bout her."

"We'll just keep praying for both of them and for their marriage. God is faithful. Sometimes we don't like his timing, but later on we can look back and see that his hand was there directing the whole time."

"Yes'um...I know that's so, but sometimes I just wish she lived close 'stead of way out yonder in California."

"I understand your concern, but I've often thought that young married couples *need* to move away from their families so they will depend on each other—not be telling all their little arguments and disagreements to their moms and dads. Nowadays, it seems like young people go into marriage with the attitude that if it doesn't work, they'll just go home to Mama, and they may not be trying hard enough to work out their differences."

"That's what I think, too, Miz Lou. Me and Ralph didn't have no family but *us*, 'cause he went to the army, and we always lived way out yonder some place all them years. But I still worry 'bout my baby girl."

"The good Lord will take care of her, Cee. Never doubt that."

An hour later, as they were finishing the last window in the second bedroom, Burt came in from his workshop.

"Good morning, Cee…how's it going? You'd better beware…Lou Ellen'll work you to death if you're not careful. Believe me, I know from experience," Burt said with his usual mischievous smile and tone.

"I would be worried, Mr. B, but you don't look no worse for wear to me…in fact, you lookin' mighty hefty these days—"

"Watch it, Cee! We don't have room for more than one comedian around here!" Burt said, making Cecily giggle.

Turning to Lou Ellen he said, "Honey, I'm going to run up to the grocery store to pick up some fresh hamburger. I'll fix lunch for the four of us…grill some burgers and make baked beans out in the patio kitchen."

"Wonderful! That will be very nice. We won't have to stop and make sandwiches, and we'll get a lot more done today."

"I thought you might like that. It'll be ready about twelve o'clock, and we'll eat on the veranda. Ralph and I are going to stop and smell the roses after lunch. The day is too beautiful to waste."

"Oh? What's on your *fun* list? What do you two have up your sleeve?" Lou Ellen asked.

"We worked this morning…we've been in the workshop making a couple of cedar bluebird houses to replace the old wooden ones that have seen their best days."

"That's work? And? This afternoon?" she pressed, grinning.

"The ponds are in great need of attention…so we are…going fishing!" Burt said with a sheepish grin. "Ralph's already down in his worm bed digging the wigglers. I'm going to swing by the bait store and get the crickets."

Cecily cackled as she said, "Mr. B, you just won't do!"

"Thank you, Cee. I'm glad *somebody* appreciates me," he said, winking at Lou Ellen.

"Well, guess what? Cecily and I aren't going to waste this beautiful day either. We refuse to be stuck in here all afternoon. We'll work an hour or so after lunch and then join you two. We'll have a fishing contest!" She said.

"All right! We'll have a fish fry for supper. It'll be *your* turn to cook!" Burt said.

"Hey! That's not fair! Cecily and I are the only two working, so you and Ralph should have to cook. Besides you know how much I hate to fry fish. But out of the goodness of my heart, I *will* make the coleslaw and hushpuppies. Deal?"

"Only if you do some cheese grits too! Deal?"

"*I'll* do the cheese grits, Mr. B," Cecily offered.

"Burt, you are such a conniver." Turning to Cecily, Lou Ellen said, "Do you realize we've just been conned?"

"Yes'um ... I believe we have, but I'll get the hot dogs out of the freezer ... just in case," she answered, grinning.

When Burt left, Cecily sighed and turned to Lou Ellen.

"Miz Lou, you told me a lot 'bout yo sad childhood one time, but you ain't ever told me how you and that good man got together. Y'all been married longer than me and Ralph, and y'all just made for each other. Tell me how you two got hitched."

"Well ... let me see ... where do I begin ... ?"

"Begin it the day you first laid eyes on him," Cecily said.

"Okay ... um ... I was a junior in high school with only about ten weeks left of school before summer vacation ... ," Lou Ellen began, as they gathered their supplies and moved to another room.

"Do you remember the friends I told you about? Amy, who showed me her cousin's pictures, and Dee, who went to church with the cousin?"

"I do ... you thought Amy's cousin was real cute, but you also thought he was too *old* for you," Cecily said.

Lou Ellen nodded and continued, "Well, financially, nothing had changed for my family. We still lived in the same four-room frame house, and I continued to walk to school every day, by way of the long gravel hill.

"One afternoon on a cold, windy day in March, I was sitting in a chair beside the wood stove in the front room doing my school homework, and I heard my daddy on the porch talking to another man. 'Do you mind if I ...' Then there were some bits and pieces of mumbled words I couldn't quite make out. Next I heard, 'Your ... daughter?' A voice I didn't recognize seemed to be questioning my daddy about *me*.

"'Yeah, sure,' I heard my daddy say, 'go on in. She's in there studyin' her lessons.'

"When the door opened and I saw the handsome man who stood there, I was shocked and utterly speechless. There stood Amy's cousin, the *sooo* cute Burt Newman, whose pictures had not done him justice. This was a dreamboat! As all six feet two inches of him strode into the room, only gravity kept me from falling off the chair! He had a jet-black Elvis hairstyle and twinkling dark eyes that said unspoken words like ... *warm, confident, happy,* and *mischief.* I thought, *Oh! My gosh! Eat your heart out, Scarlett O'Hara.*"

"Ooh! That's so exciting!" Cecily interjected. "Sorry I interrupted! Go on, Miz Lou."

Smiling at Cecily's enthusiasm, she continued. "Burt'd come to ask my daddy's permission to date me! I thought, *Shouldn't he have asked me first?* But he already knew I was interested in him. Dee had a big mouth! Burt told me later that Dee'd told him at church that I'd shown an interest in dating him. But I was so shocked when he showed up at my house I'm not sure I even asked him to sit down!

"That afternoon, we made plans to have a first date a couple of nights later. We planned to go to a revival at a church close by, so that my daddy'd give me permission to go out. There weren't many places he'd allow me to go, except church. But it wouldn't have mattered to me *where* we went. I thought I was already in love, and I just wanted to be *with* him."

"You fell in love with his good looks! What's that song that girl sings...the first time I looked at you...or somethin' like that?" Cecily asked.

"Oh yeah...you're probably thinking about 'The First Time Ever I Saw Your Face.'"

"That's the one!"

"I *love* that song. It hadn't been released then, but now it certainly applies to how I felt that afternoon all those years ago. Later, Burt told me he'd fallen in love with me that same night he'd picked me up for our first date, and that I was so beautiful in '*that dress.*'

"I remember it vividly. My outfit was a navy blue velveteen fitted jumper that Burt also told me showed off my cute figure to a tee! Underneath, I wore a light blue long-sleeved blouse with flowing chiffon sleeves. I'd made the jumper in my Home Economics class; the material had been a gift from my teacher, and I silently thanked Miss Daniels again.

"From that first afternoon, my days were never the same. Burt treated me with the utmost respect. He told me his mom'd always told him to treat any girl he dated just like he'd want a sister of his to be treated, and he was a perfect gentleman with me.

"My daddy approved of Burt right from the start because he knew Burt was a Christian and was teaching a Sunday school class at his church. Even my mother liked him, because he teased her a lot, and she enjoyed the attention.

"When Burt and I began dating, I had a kitten someone had given me that I'd named Missy. Missy always came running to the car when we drove into the driveway after a date. I'd open my door and Missy'd jump in and walk back and forth across the back of the seat between Burt and me, purring and begging for attention.

"On our third date, after we said goodnight and started to get out of the car for Burt to walk me to the door, Missy walked across the seat to Burt, and I reached for her. As I did, Burt pulled me close and kissed me for the first time. It was sooo sweet, and if I wasn't already, I fell head over heels at that moment! I'd touched his face with my hand when he kissed me, and I remember going to bed that night and falling asleep with my hands cupped around my nose to keep the smell of his after-shave cologne close."

"That love bug bit you *good*, didn't it, Miz Lou?"

"It sure did, Cee!" Lou Ellen said, laughing. "I didn't know then that Burt didn't particularly like cats. Later he cheekily said, 'I loved that cat!' Now that I think about it, he actually did grow fond of Missy."

Lou Ellen stood and stretched her arms and shoulder muscles. "Let's take a break for a few minutes, have a cup of coffee and a ginger snap or two ... what do you say?"

"Sounds good to me, Miz Lou, but don't stop tellin' yo story. It's just gettin' to the good part. What happened next?"

After they sat down with the coffee and cookies, Lou Ellen continued.

"From that first date, I don't think a day passed that Burt and I didn't see each other at some point during the day, or *several* times a day. Driving his mom's car, he came in the mornings and took me to school, picked me up in the afternoons, and took me home or wherever I was scheduled or just wanted to go. He came to my house most nights, even if we weren't planning to go out. Sometimes we just sat and talked, and other times he helped me practice my parts in the upcoming school play. If Burt stayed too long at night when he came to see me, my daddy'd say, 'Burt, it's time to go home now.' He did. If we stayed in the car in the driveway too long when we got home from a date, my daddy'd come to the door and say, 'It's time to come in, Lou Ellen.' I did. We abided by all the rules. We just wanted to be together, and abiding by the rules made it possible.

"And Burt was there waiting for me when I left Dixie Belle's Cafe on Sundays after church. We'd go to visit his parents or cousins or just drive around in his car listening to music. We listened to songs by Marty Robbins, Jerry Lee Lewis, Eddie Arnold, Jim Reeves, the Everly Brothers, and many more. But our favorite song was 'Send Me the Pillow That You Dream On,' sung by

Hank Locklin. We talked endlessly and were content just being together. For the first time in my life, I was not embarrassed by the way we lived. Burt didn't care a whit about my unpainted house, the oil lamp, or the outhouse. *He'd* lived in dilapidated shanties too. He just loved me! And he told me so over and over. Every day with Burt was a good day, and every day I fell more in love with him. My lonely past was just that—past! Burt was not only handsome, he was a Christian, fun loving, and terribly witty; and best of all, he *loved me*. What more could I ask for?"

"That's enough, Miz Lou. You had all you needed. I hope you didn't go asking the good Lord for more!"

Smiling she said, "No, I didn't, but there *was* more, Cee. Burt was romantic. He loved Elizabeth Barrett Browning, especially her 'How Do I Love Thee?' poem, and he often recited it to me. He wrote me love poems, and we often wrote and mailed each other love letters, even though we saw each other daily."

"Oh, Miz Lou, that's sooo sweet. I love a tenderhearted romantic man. My Ralph's sweet like that too, but he don't know no poetry," Cecily said.

"I know it sounds old fashioned . . . even corny, Cee, but the absolute truth is it *was* love at first sight for me. He was my Romeo, my best friend, my knight in shining armor, my hero, and my soul mate."

"Ain't nothin' corny 'bout a love like that! That rascal done stole yo heart right outta yo chest for sure, Miz Lou."

"Yes he had! I began to feel like Cinderella. All I lacked were the glass slippers!"

"Well . . . last time I vacuumed that big walk-in closet you got now, I didn't see no *room* for no more shoes—not even them famous glass ones!" Cecily teased, and Lou Ellen laughed.

"And now I think this is a good place to take a bathroom break and then get back to our window washing," she said as they rinsed their coffee cups and got up to move their supplies to the den.

"So, what was Mr. B's family like, Miz Lou?" Cecily asked.

"Burt's parents, Calvin and Wilma, became the traditional, dependable, inwardly *and* outwardly loving parents I'd never had. I loved my daddy, but he could be there today and gone tomorrow, so the security I needed was tenuous, at best. Nor did I know then, or for many *years,* how much my daddy truly did love me.

"Burt's childhood was totally different from mine. While we were dating, when we went to his house for supper, which was often, his mom entertained me with tales of his childhood antics, much to his chagrin at times. She had a wonderful sense of humor and was a great storyteller, with a tendency to embellish. *Their* house was *fun!*

"His family had always been sharecroppers, so they were poor too, but Burt never realized they were poor. Wilma and several other mothers in Cloverton always carpooled and worked at one of several textile factories located in different surrounding towns—shirt factories, linen factories, and the likes—in order to supplement the meager family income. So Burt's mom kept him supplied with clothes and spending money for toys, movies, or whatever else he needed or wanted. Burt's happiness always came first with his parents.

"Our families knew each other and both lived in Cloverton, but his family had always lived out in the country because his dad farmed. They'd moved to Ashville during Burt's last three years of high school, and then they moved back to Cloverton during his senior year. Burt commuted in order to graduate with his classmates in Ashville. Consequently, I didn't know him.

"By the time Burt and I met, his family was living in a white house with all the conveniences, plus extras such as a washing machine and a television, and Burt drove his mom's almost new car all the time. Burt helped his dad on the farm after he graduated from high school, but then he left home to spend six months active duty in a military reserve field. When we met he had come back home again to help his dad.

"Right from the beginning, I felt that Burt's mom and dad loved me very much, and I dearly loved them. Burt's parents knew how strict my daddy was and knew his health history as well, but they accepted and loved me anyway. His mom was also clever; she included my daddy and mother in a lot of the suppers at her house. How could they refuse to let me go when they were invited too? After we ate, we always watched Mom's favorite western on TV every Saturday night, and she'd often pretend to swoon when the handsome male star of the show appeared on the screen. There was never a dull moment at Burt's mom and dad's house."

"When did Mr. B propose, and where were you when he popped the question?" Cecily asked.

"Burt never proposed to me in the traditional style. He didn't need to. We both just knew we'd be married one day. We talked about 'when we get married.' When we asked my daddy to sign for me to get a marriage license, he didn't exactly refuse. 'Wait a while,' he said without further explanation.

"Not knowing exactly how long my daddy's 'Wait a while' meant, we continued with preparations. I bought a pretty blue dress because there wasn't a white one to be found in our town, and we didn't have money for a fancy wedding anyway. We'd had the mandatory blood tests done…thinking we'd ask my pastor to marry us in a simple, private ceremony. My daddy knew about the preparations because my mother had gone with us to get the blood tests, and she'd seen the dress too.

"Time passed. When I asked Daddy again, he still simply said, 'Wait a while.' I couldn't understand the big deal and Daddy's reluctance to sign. I wasn't planning to quit school. I planned to finish my junior year and go back in the fall and get my diploma. But my daddy didn't mention that or give any reason for his delay in signing. I didn't know what his problem was! Everything was crystal clear to Burt and me, so we got frustrated. I began to think maybe all our preparations were wasted, but giving blood for naught was a very big deal to Burt! I remember he nearly passed out the day we had our blood tests done. I didn't know it then, but Burt had an idea cooking in his head."

At that moment, Burt opened the door and announced lunch.

"We'll be right there," Lou Ellen said.

"Don't forget where you left off. I can't wait to hear the rest of this story, Miz Lou," Cecily said as they joined the men on the veranda.

CHAPTER SEVENTEEN

With stomachs full of burgers and beans, Lou Ellen and Cecily stood in the den and debated whether to take a nap or finish their chores. Cecily suggested they keep working so she could find out the solution to the marriage license predicament. Lou Ellen decided they'd move all their supplies into the kitchen, a room with fewer windows so they'd be done in an hour to join the men at the pond. Tomorrow they'd do the master suite, which was the largest and most time-consuming area, plus the bathrooms and the office. They'd done the sunroom a couple of weeks earlier, so it wasn't on the list this time. After they got started working again, Cecily turned to Lou Ellen.

"Okay, Miz Lou, I wanna hear the rest of yo story. How'd you convince yo daddy to sign for you and Mr. B to be married?"

"Well … Burt's mom and dad were good, fun-loving folks, and they had a lot of friends. Wilma had a heart of gold and was a giving, loving person. She drew people like a magnet because everybody just thoroughly enjoyed merely being around her. But his mom and dad had spoiled Burt beyond redemption! Whatever Burt wanted, he got!"

"That boy must've been rotten."

"That'd be an understatement, if everything his mom told me was for real, and Burt doesn't deny any of it. She'd tell tales of his little temper tantrums, lying down in the floor, screaming to get his way until she gave in. She said he was so headstrong she'd just finally give up, and that when she did whip him, it broke her heart and she cried more than he did. But he outgrew all that nonsense and turned out fine, don't you think, Cee?"

"Yes'um, Miz Lou, I'd say he's a keeper."

"Anyway … Burt wanted me for his wife! He knew his mom would help with his problem. When he told her about the marriage license situation with my daddy, she took matters into her own hands. She knew and was friends with a lot of the people at the courthouse in Pikeville, a town twenty miles away that was the county seat where the marriage licenses had to be obtained. So Burt and his mom, Wilma, drove to the Pikeville courthouse. Later he told me about that nerve-wracking experience.

"He said when they entered the courthouse, Wanda, his mom's longtime friend, was one of the ladies working that day. He said she had a loud, jolly voice that could be heard all over the room … and probably down the hall. She hurried around the counter to give his mom a hug, saying, 'Well, bless my soul, Wilma! I haven't seen you in a month of Sundays. I almost didn't know you.'

"'Good morning, Wanda, how're you this morning? It's so good to see you. You remember my son, Burt?' his mom said.

"'Yes, of course I do, Wilma. It's good to see you both. Burt, it has been even longer since I've seen *you*. Your mama told me you went into the military for a while,' Wanda said as she hugged him too.

"'Yes, ma'am, but I'm home now and planning to get married,' Burt told her.

"'Oh, heck! I was hoping you'd wait until my little Teresa grows up … she's thirteen now, you know,' Wanda teased him. Burt said she was hoping to make him blush, and she succeeded and kept on talking.

"'And Wilma, what has been keeping you away so long? You were supposed to come have lunch with me one day!'

"'Well, you know how it is … the road is paved with good intentions. Busy seems to be my middle name, and right now we're sort of in a hurry. I need to sign for Burt to get a marriage license, since he is only nineteen, and I need to pick up one for his fiancée, Lou Ellen Hudson, also,' his mom told her.

"'Okay … no problem. Just give me a few minutes, and y'all can be on your way. By the way, congratulations, Burt! I wish you the best,' Wanda said, hurrying away.

"Burt said his mouth was almost too dry to get one more word out, but he'd managed to say, 'Thanks.'

"A short time later, they walked out of the courthouse with the marriage licenses. His mom said it'd been a piece of cake! Burt told me *he'd* been a nervous wreck, but then he told me he was a nervous wreck that afternoon when he came to ask me for a date too. Knowing him now, that's hard to believe, isn't it, Cee?"

"It is indeed, Miz Lou. That man don't act like he's *ever* had a case of nerves. Go on now ... I can't wait to hear the rest of this. I'm 'bout to get a case of nerves myself!"

"Okay, okay ... Burt came to my house early the next morning. It was my first day of summer vacation. Burt told me about getting the license with his mom's help. Since we'd been waiting for my daddy's approval and signature, we hadn't set a wedding date. We sat there and made plans for the following morning.

"Two and one half months after we met, we eloped!"

"*Ooh* ... Miz Lou, I'm so nervous for y'all ... I'm about to have a case of the vapors—as my mama used to say when she felt faint! How'd y'all do it?" Cecily said, fanning herself.

Laughing out loud, Lou Ellen said, "Oh, calm down, Cecily. That was nearly half a century ago!"

"But I keep *forgettin'* that part ... go on!"

"On our wedding day, Burt picked me up to drive me around as he usually did. I'd already put some of my clothes and my wedding dress in a bag. I'd told my mother and daddy I was going to Granny Simpson's house to sew on her old pedal sewing machine, which I often did. On our way out of town, we stopped and told Granny what was happening. We asked her to wait until late that afternoon, and then she could go tell my daddy we'd eloped, so he wouldn't worry when we didn't come home. We went to Burt's house and got dressed while his mom tried to encourage us and keep us both calm. We drove to the courthouse here in Valley Lake, and instead of a justice of the peace, we were married by a reverend. They told us he *just happened* to be in the courthouse at that precise moment, but I didn't ever believe that was just a coincidence.

"At last it was official. We were now Mr. and Mrs. Burt Newman! For a honeymoon we went to Pensacola, Florida, for two nights—that's all we could afford—and we visited some of Burt's relatives who lived in that area. My life with Burt began the exact opposite of my lonely childhood. As Mrs. Lou Ellen Newman, I woke up each morning excited and eager to start a new day...a new *life*. My joy was complete, and Burt made me happy to the core of my being."

"Oh! Miz Lou, what happened with your daddy? Was he mad at y'all?" Cecily asked, concern on her face as though it was currently happening.

"No, but my daddy did *not* take the news of our elopement well. When Burt and I went back to my house on Sunday to get my clothes, he was inside, lying on the couch. My mother told me he'd been lying there since Granny Simpson told him we'd eloped, only getting up occasionally. I went alone into the living room where he was, knelt down beside the couch, and apologized for making him sad, cried with him, hugged him, and told him I loved him, but that I loved Burt too. Daddy was not mad, just deeply depressed. But all that changed. He grew to love Burt almost as much as I do."

Placing her cleaning supplies in the basket, Lou Ellen said, "And now it's time for a change for both of us...all work and no play—"

"Makes Miz Lou and Cee dull girls!" Cecily finished for her. "That's such a sweet love story, Miz Lou. Thanks for sharing it with me. And I agree...it's time to play. Let's go join the men folk!"

CHAPTER EIGHTEEN

A couple of weeks went by before Lou Ellen had another
night of insomnia and went out for her usual therapy
on the veranda; listening to the soothing, mesmerizing
fountain and the sounds of the outdoor night life. She and Burt
had spent several late afternoons on the patio watching the birds
until dusk, but they hadn't seen Little Red for the past two weeks.
Now she stood scanning the shadows, but it was rather cloudy, and
she couldn't see well enough ... even if he *was* there. Occasionally
the clouds floated over and the moon peeped through, but for
only seconds. She was beginning to be concerned about Little
Red, and she hoped she'd be able to see him before she went back
inside. She always got upset when she heard a hawk outside near
the bird feeder because she had seen one take a bird more than
once. Burt told her she had to remember that it was nature's way;
it wasn't as though she could protect the wild things like they
were her house pets. But she often wished she could.

As was the case the last time she went out there during a
sleepless night, her mind began to wander to her past; but she
was at peace with her memories lately. She thought it was probably because she had reached the point in her recollections when
she was no longer alone, when she had more love than she'd ever
imagined. Now the majority of her memories were happy ones
shared with the love of her life, and later, their children. And
many of her happy memories were of Burt's parents, Mom and
Dad Newman.

After they came back from their honeymoon, Burt continued to
help his dad on the farm; and, as he and his mom and dad had
discussed and agreed upon, Lou Ellen and Burt lived with them.

They spent a memorable summer going fishing, going to movies, listening to music, attending Burt's church and sometimes visiting hers. In *her* opinion she made some really cute clothes using Mom Newman's sewing machine, getting ready for her senior year of high school. That summer Lou Ellen celebrated her seventeenth birthday with her new family, and it was the first birthday cake and celebration she'd ever had.

A few days before school started, Mom confided in her how much she wanted a better life for Burt and her than a sharecropper career offered. She told Lou Ellen she should encourage Burt to look for a job in a larger city where there were more opportunities. Lou Ellen attended only one day of her senior year of high school because while she was in school that day, Burt went job hunting in Louiston, a city fifty miles away. He was hired immediately, and they asked him to start work as soon as possible. The next day they went apartment hunting and moved to Louiston.

Their first home was a furnished one-room apartment above the garage of a large white house with a big yard and many trees. Separated from the main house by a long, glass-enclosed breezeway, it was cozy and private. One corner of the room had been enclosed where a bathroom was built, but the remainder was all open. A tiny kitchenette occupied the remaining area beside the bathroom and contained a small breakfast table. The rest was a living and sleeping area, with a bed on one side and a couch and small closet on the other. A washer and dryer in the garage below was an added blessing since the landlady told Lou Ellen she was welcome to use them. She loved everything about their first "home."

Mom Newman was right there the next day to help her decorate, and she brought a pretty bedspread and a curtain for the one tiny window located over the sink in the kitchenette. When they finished decorating the apartment, Mom took her on her first grocery shopping trip and helped her remember what she might need to cook her husband's first meal in their new home. Again Mom confided in her.

"Lou Ellen, it broke my heart to see you and Burt packing your things to move yesterday."

"I know, Mom. I got teary when we said good-bye too."

"But I know it's for the best. There are no opportunities for a young married couple in a small town like Cloverton," Mom continued, starting to tear up again.

"We'll go back to see you all the time; I promise. Don't cry, or I'll be crying with you."

"Well, I did feel better after I reminded myself y'all would only be an hour away, and we could visit each other often."

And we drove home to be with them nearly every weekend, because Mom gave us her car to make it possible, she thought.

To Lou Ellen, that little garage apartment was a castle. She loved being a wife and homemaker, and she was striving to become a good cook. Mom had taught her a lot about cooking over the summer. Most of all, she couldn't wait to start a family and be a mother. But God, in his infinite wisdom, had other plans.

They'd lived in their little garage apartment about a year when Burt was promoted to manager of the business where he worked. One of the perks of the promotion was a three-bedroom brick home located right beside the business, rent-free. They bought their own furniture and appliances on payment plan. Things couldn't get much better.

She and Burt often looked back and laughed at silly things they'd said and done during their first year or two as newlyweds. Burt particularly loved teasing her about the time his mom and dad had given them a pig to have processed for their freezer. He told Lou Ellen to write down instructions as to how she wanted it packaged, and he'd take it to the slaughterhouse with him. Burt told her he didn't look at her list, so he was surprised when the man handling his order started to laugh, until he handed the paper back to him. Her list had included: ten packages of bacon, ten packages of pork chops, one ham, one roast, and the remainder in hamburger meat! When he got home, he didn't waste any time. He began to tease her.

"*Hamburger* comes from a *cow,* honey." Burt told her, slowly enunciating each word.

"Well, *excuse* me! I did not know. We never had cow at our house!" she said, mimicking his tone.

"I know you've never lived on a farm, but you should learn the difference between beef and pork," he said.

"And maybe *you* should learn how to cook it too!" she said while thinking, *Smart aleck!*

"My! My! Aren't we feisty?" Burt replied, a grin threatening the corner of his mouth while already dancing in his eyes. He knew all the right buttons to push to see the fire in hers, and he pushed them often. Even knowing that about him, Lou Ellen frequently fell into his trap, and she could see he'd accomplished his goal again.

"Burt, be honest now … isn't it logical that if a ham comes from a pig, one would think ham-*burger* should too?" she said, smiling and speaking slowly with exaggerated sweetness. He finally gave up.

Then a cloud appeared on the horizon. While they lived in the brick house in Louiston, Lou Ellen's daddy became sick again. Eventually he went into the deeply depressed state, and she and Burt brought him to stay with them. One day he told Lou Ellen he wanted to "go back up yonder," which was the institution he always went to. He seemed to sense when he wasn't going to get any better until he went back there for a while. She and Burt took him there, but that time Burt was her rock, her strength. She'd not felt physically all alone.

Daniel was gone for a few weeks again. Meanwhile, back in Cloverton, Lena had already moved back in with Granny Simpson. When Daniel went home, he and Lena rented a house just four houses away from Granny Simpson. At long last, the Hudsons finally lived in town, in the painted white house with all the conveniences Lou Ellen had always wanted for them. And her daddy was fine for a while.

While they lived in the brick house by Burt's business, Jeremy and Sue lived with Burt and Lou Ellen for a few weeks during Jeremy's job-related transfer and move to Louiston. Lou Ellen and Sue thought a spotless home was a mandatory requirement to qualify as a good wife. They spent their time cleaning house, down on their hands and knees waxing all the hardwood floors, going grocery shopping, cooking, and then just "playing."

They often went to a popular park and swimming hole on the outskirts of town, where they'd learned to swim—*sort of.* Neither of them could swim well, but they bravely played around in the deepest part anyway. One day while holding onto the side, Sue turned loose, lost her confidence, and panicked. Before Lou Ellen had time to panic too—*because she certainly could not have saved her*—in a flash, the lifeguard dove in right beside Sue and saved the day! Lou Ellen was sure he'd been well trained about novice swimmers' youthful lack of fear, and maybe lack of common sense as well.

They'd had a few other questionably intelligent experiences back in those early days of their friendship. Since Burt worked right next door, Lou Ellen always had their car—no driver's license yet—but she drove everywhere anyway. Mom had taught her to drive her stick shift car when she and Burt got married. She and Sue often drove back to Cloverton to visit family for a day, or sometimes just to eat lunch with Sue's mom.

One day, from somewhere or someone, Sue got the bright idea that the two of them needed to take some medicine she'd heard about that "cleans you out and makes your insides like new; and you just feel so much better… all over." Lou Ellen couldn't remember what the medicine was called. She didn't *want* to!

They were going to visit Sue's mom for lunch, and for some odd reason they chose that particular day to take the medicine. Before they left for Cloverton, they both took twice the amount recommended, because Sue said, "If a little is good, twice as much will be even better." So, by the time they arrived in Cloverton, Lou Ellen was totally I-just-want-to-die *sick*. She would always remember the sink and the toilet in Sue's mom's bathroom were close together, which was an excellent thing. She repeatedly used both at the same time while wishing she was already dead! Sue wasn't quite as sick and must have driven them home. Lou Ellen was too sick to remember the minor stuff. She occasionally still reminded Sue about the time she'd nearly killed her!

Probably the most dangerous thing they'd done together was drag race on a highway that, for the most part, was in an undeveloped area at the time. It was a divided four-lane with few and far between traffic lights that were far enough apart they could drag and race from light to light quite successfully. They both loved it, and plenty of others must have too because they always found somebody willing to accommodate—some other daredevil who just happened to come up to the red light at the same time they did. In those days when they floored the accelerator to drag, their age group called it "scratching off," as opposed to "peeling out" or "burning rubber." *Bless poor Burt and Jeremy's hearts!* She thought. *They were working their behinds off while Sue and I burned up the road… and their tires!*

She didn't know about Sue, but *she* still had a little remnant remaining of that lust for speed from those days. *Ooh… what fun we had back then!* Little did she know *then* that a seemingly few short years later her youngest son would follow in her footsteps! And she'd not had nearly as much fun then.

By the time Lou Ellen went to get her driver's license, Sue had started working, and Jeremy took her to take the test. At least with her license she and Sue were legal when they were doing those daring things, even though it didn't make the act itself legal or any safer. Truthfully, she didn't think she'd even told Burt about some of those questionable stunts at the time. *In those days, God surely had his hands full with us at times,* she thought.

Jake was Burt's coworker who owned a boat, and she and Burt sometimes went to the Chattahoochee River to water ski with Jake and his wife, Vicki. One Sunday afternoon, for whatever reason, Vicki didn't go. After Burt drove the boat for Jake to ski, and vice versa, they were bored.

"Man, I wish Vicki could've come," Burt said. "I miss skiing together like we usually do."

"I know; so do I, but we'll come back another week. And I'll make sure Vicki—"

"I have an idea … let *me* drive the boat," Lou Ellen interrupted, getting excited at the prospect and adding, "*Please … pretty please.*"

"Uh … uh—," Jake began at precisely the moment when Burt was saying, "No … I don't think that would be a good idea for—"

"Oh! You two! Don't be such dodos … let me drive the boat," Lou Ellen said. "I know exactly how. I've been watching you two and Vicki drive all these times … I can do it!" she added with confidence. *What wimps!* she thought.

After a good bit more begging, they finally agreed to let her try, but with much reluctance and little confidence. They showed her the hand signals they would use to communicate with her and what each meant: the "go faster," the "slow down," and the "rest a while." When they were tired, they were going to give her the "rest a while" signal, which meant they wanted to ski into the designated white sandy beach area located on a straight stretch, just after a curve in the river.

They headed out, and things went better than even she'd expected. They skied several rounds, giving her the "slower" signal when they approached the curve, and the "faster" signal after coming out of the curve into the straight stretch that passed the designated landing spot. The "faster" signal was the fun one. She *loved* speed!

She did a good job too … until the "rest a while" signal. They failed to tell her to slow down after she cleared the curve so that they could just smoothly and slowly ski right up onto the sandy bank. The key word was *slowly. They may have thought I was smart enough to know to slow down, not speed up as usual!*

Burt and Jake were crossing over the wake, angled toward shore, when Lou Ellen hit the throttle full blast, just as she had been doing all the other times after they came out of the curve. When they hit the sand at high speed on those skis, simultaneously Burt and Jake did a perfectly choreographed, double cartwheel onto the landing beach. Lou Ellen thought that was the neatest, funniest thing she'd ever seen performed. *They* failed to see the humor! *Some people just don't have any sense of humor!* she thought, laughing out loud as she remembered that scene.

It was her grand, solo performance in more ways than one. She'd never driven a boat before, and she was sure she never would again if Jake and Burt had any say-so! And she was right! Though they hadn't trusted her to drive the boat again, by God's good graces, neither Burt nor Jake was hurt. Lou Ellen survived their wrath too, but she'd had her doubts for a few seconds.

CHAPTER NINETEEN

The 1960s brought many changes for Burt and Lou Ellen. Burt started taking college classes, changed career fields, and landed a job with a large electronics firm. Over the years he'd steadily advanced the ladder of success and eventually became a field consultant. His job took them far away, in other states and sometimes other countries for several years. They enjoyed traveling and living in new places, and life was good. But it hadn't all been trouble free.

When Lou Ellen didn't get pregnant for nearly two years, she prayed and prayed for a baby, and a year later God blessed them with a healthy, nine-pound baby boy they named Kevin. That was the day that she discovered a mother can love her child more than anything on earth, including herself. She learned the true meaning of "a miracle from God." *We were so happy,* she thought.

A year and a half later, while living in Indianapolis, Lou Ellen became pregnant again, and they were even *happier!* About six weeks into the pregnancy, they went back to Cloverton on vacation, and while there she began having complications with the pregnancy. She went to her childhood family doctor, who prescribed total bed rest and told her she shouldn't travel for a few weeks. She spent the week in bed, and everything seemed okay. When she went back for a checkup, she told the doctor she didn't want to be separated from Burt and wanted to go back home with him. Dr. Baxter told her if she was determined to travel, then she should make the trip lying in the back seat and that they should certainly stay the night near a hospital, just in case. They started the trip back to Indiana, and about halfway home on Friday night they stayed in a motel in a town near Nashville.

Early in the morning, Lou Ellen went into labor, and Burt called an ambulance to take her to the small hospital there.

Thinking she had miscarried, the doctor on duty performed the common minor surgery necessary, but her condition continued to worsen. Burt was staying in the motel with eighteen-month old Kevin, but when he went to the hospital to visit her, the nurses would not allow Kevin to go into her room with him. When they tried to hold Kevin for Burt to go in alone, he screamed at the top of his lungs because they were strangers to him. Lou Ellen could hear him screaming down the hall, couldn't stand to hear him crying, so Burt had to leave and calm him down. Consequently, she and Burt only had a few five-minute visits.

After two days in the hospital and going steadily down-hill—to the point she was being given blood transfusions—Lou Ellen was transferred on Sunday night to the Baptist Hospital in Nashville, where she received emergency surgery for a ruptured tubal pregnancy.

The night the ambulance transferred her, Burt was on his way to visit her and passed the ambulance going the opposite direction, away from the hospital with its siren on. He said he didn't know *how*, but he just *knew* she was on that ambulance, and he'd almost followed it without checking with the hospital first; his feeling was that strong.

Burt had a stressful week, and Lou Ellen was concerned for him and for her toddler, who wasn't old enough to understand. He'd had to leave her alone in the hospital and drive the last half of the trip home the next day—alone with a toddler. Then he found a sitter, reported to work every day, and drove back to get her the following weekend. She didn't know anyone in the Nashville area, so she didn't have a single visitor all week, but Burt's mom called the hospital to check on her every day. She told the nurse who answered to be sure to go to Lou Ellen's room and tell her that her mom had called and that she was praying for her.

And once again... God took care of us all, she thought.

While not normally a worrier, after a year passed and she didn't get pregnant again, Lou Ellen began to worry that with only one fallopian tube, she would never have another baby; and she was deeply saddened. Initially she and Burt had wanted to have three children, and *again* she prayed and prayed. God graciously answered those prayers too. A year later, they were blessed with another healthy, nine-pound baby boy they named Ryan. He was yet another miracle from God. *And we were so proud.*

Burt's mom was Lou Ellen's greatest mentor after her teenage years. Mom was always there for her even after they moved far away. When they went home on vacation or holidays, they stayed at Mom and Dad's house, even though her own daddy and mother lived in the same town. And Mom always included her mother and daddy in all the Thanksgiving, Christmas, and regular Sunday dinners at her house, so they could be with them too. Mom and Dad Newman's home was really small, but Mom's heart was big enough for everybody.

When she and Burt had been married eight years and had their two small children, Burt spent a job-related year overseas. Since Kevin was about to start kindergarten, Lou Ellen and the boys stayed with Burt's mom and dad, who had moved to West Palm, Florida. One day Mom came home from work and told Lou Ellen she wanted to discuss something with her.

"I've been thinking that you might want to go back to school to get your diploma, and this would be an ideal time while Burt is working out of the country and you're living with us."

"How can I possibly do that? Kevin is only in kindergarten for half a day, and Ryan—"

"One of my clients told me about a night program they have at the high school here. You would get a regular diploma next spring just like the seniors. You could enroll in that, and I will be home from work to keep the boys while you attend classes," she said.

"That sounds good, but—"

"I'll pay for Ryan to go to the daycare where Kevin goes to kindergarten. That way your mornings will be free so that you can study," Mom said.

"Mom, that would make me so happy, but I don't know how to find out what subjects I need, or how—"

"All you have to do is go enroll. They'll contact your high school back in Cloverton and get your transcripts and tell you what subjects and how many credits you need to graduate," Mom said, enjoying Lou Ellen's obvious excitement.

Lou Ellen enrolled and after the school received her transcripts from Cloverton, they told Lou Ellen she only needed two credits to graduate—Psychology and English Literature—so her schedule was *easy*. She attended classes for two hours at night and studied every morning; but she cleaned, did laundry, and cooked dinner in the afternoons. When she received her diploma, it was hard to tell who was more proud—Mom or her!

Almost a decade later Lou Ellen attended college classes, majored in computer science, and eventually became an award-winning systems analyst while employed with the U.S. Government. It saddened her that Mom didn't live to know the whole story. Lou Ellen felt her achievements were, in part, because of *her*, and she would have been so proud. Mom passed away suddenly at the young age of sixty while Lou Ellen and Burt were living abroad. She and the children had not been able to fly home with Burt, but Mom would always have a special and permanent place in Lou Ellen's heart.

The sad thoughts of never having been able to say good-bye to Mom Newman prompted Lou Ellen to realize the time. She picked up the night-vision goggles, scanned the yard, the cat food bowls, and the bird feeders. Seeing nothing, she placed them back on the table and went inside. She wasn't sleepy, but maybe she'd just read for a while.

CHAPTER TWENTY

Lou Ellen was lying in her recliner, watching a movie on television. The story was about a young woman whose father was stricken with Alzheimer's disease, and she went back home to help. She'd seen it before, but there wasn't anything else on tonight that interested her. In fact, Burt was of the same opinion and had gone to bed early. Before long, the TV screen began to blur, and Lou Ellen's memories came flooding back.

A few years after Lou Ellen and Burt moved away from Cloverton, they went back home for a vacation. Right away she detected her daddy was showing signs of the onset of his illness, so she scheduled a consultation appointment with their family doctor to discuss her daddy's illness and options. She asked him questions about a possible brain tumor or other medical condition he might possibly have that could cause his mood swings. But basically, the doctor gave her no encouragement or hope for her daddy's condition or prognosis.

During the next few years, each time Lou Ellen got the call her daddy was sick, if at all possible she drove or flew home, depending on where they were living. If she was out of the country or could not go home for some other reason, her mother's family always handled it for her. Her life had been busy furthering her education, being a wife and mother, and living away from it all. *Now I realize just how much they did to help and how much I appreciate them,* she thought.

When she *was* able to go home, most of the time she just took her daddy to the doctor, who got him started on medicines. She stayed a week and monitored his meds and food to get him on the road to recovery. Other times he would have to be hospitalized for several days in Louiston because he was prone to get phlebitis in one of his legs. It would be swollen, discolored, and painful, and it was often the result of his being on his feet and constantly overly active for nearly twenty-four hours a day.

While her daddy was in the hospital for problems with his leg, the doctor would also start him on medicines for his mental condition, and he always began to get better. Lou Ellen cooked, cleaned, and drove back and forth to the hospital and took her mother to see him daily. When they allowed him to go home, he had to have total bed rest for his leg, which meant he got a lot of attention, and Lou Ellen made sure he followed the doctor's orders. Invariably, by the time the week was up, her mother started to act sicker than her daddy because *he* was getting all the attention.

If Lou Ellen lived close enough and had driven there instead of flying, she often took her daddy back home with her, depending on his ability to travel. Usually if he'd been hospitalized for his leg, he was physically unable to go home with her. As long as Granny Simpson was alive, her mother would not come with him. The source of her mother's personal security was with her own mother.

It was during one of those episodes many years later that Lou Ellen learned her daddy's illness was called manic-depressive disorder, and even later came to be known as bipolar disorder. But in those early dark days of her childhood, no one knew about the term *manic-depressive* illness or how to best treat it. It was just known as mental illness, which carried a certain stigma, usually resulting in even more certain incarceration. It was also then that her daddy told her what really happened when he "went up yonder" to the institution. He was given shock treatments. Though shock therapy was controversial, it was a common practice for severe depression in mental hospitals when Lou Ellen was a child. They were given while the patient was fully awake and aware through the entire procedure and were often given three times a week. It was reported that sometimes the convulsions that resulted from shock therapy were severe enough to break bones. Her daddy's description of those horrible times was hard to hear, and her heart ached for him.

Lou Ellen knew that she could do things to help her parents, and she did whatever she could. But there were other situations she had no control over. It was frustrating, but she eventually had to learn to accept them.

Her daddy had been sick, had gone to the state hospital again, and Lou Ellen had brought him to stay with them when he was released. One of Daniel's doctors at the institution wrote her a letter after his release, suggesting her daddy needed to move permanently away from Cloverton for the good of his mental health. He said he needed to live in a positive environment in order to control his emotional fluctuations, and he gave several additional reasons. Burt and Lou Ellen intended to have him continue to live with them; however, as soon as he seemed fully recovered, he talked constantly of going home. He loved his wife, felt responsible for her, and said she *needed* him. He did not want to live away from Lena, but *she* wanted to live with, or very near, her own mother. Besides, when her daddy was not sick, he was content in Cloverton and loved living there. It was home to him, and he was happy there.

Lou Ellen was between a rock and a hard place! There was nothing she could do. Eventually her daddy went back to Cloverton, and he and Lena moved permanently into the same house with Granny Simpson. Granny's apartment was on one side of a long, wide hallway, and Daniel and Lena's was on the other side. Each had their own kitchen and bedrooms, but they shared a bath off the hallway in between.

Okay... enough of these kinds of memories. I've had too many good ones I'd rather spend my time on, Lou Ellen thought as she turned off the television and went to bed.

CHAPTER TWENTY-ONE

Burt loved to hear Lou Ellen laugh and would go to great lengths to make her laugh until she cried, which he took even greater pleasure in. He'd get tickled at her laughing, and then she'd laugh even more at *him*. It was a vicious circle because as long as it worked, he kept it up. There was no end to his clowning antics. But years ago there was one occasion when he hadn't needed to clown to make her laugh.

Although it took no small amount of persuasion, Burt reluctantly agreed to go to a Halloween party in their neighborhood as a *female* character! Because he could imitate her perfectly, Lou Ellen dressed him as "Geraldine," the girlfriend of the black TV comedian, Flip Wilson. She bought his costume from a used clothing store … a hot pink dress that she shortened to six inches above his knees. She was positive that no wife has truly lived until she has seen her husband's extremely knobby knees in a hot pink mini dress, wearing black nylons, size *twelve* ladies' high heels, the darkest make-up available, and a blonde wig. She laughed until tears rolled down her cheeks … until he threatened to stay home! The sight of him carrying a big purse and trying to walk down the sidewalk in high heels was even funnier, but she didn't dare let him see her laugh. She really wanted to go to that party.

Not to worry! When they arrived, he morphed; he *became* Geraldine, entertained the crowd, and had a blast. Silly her, she just *thought* he was shy! Oh what a fun-loving clown he really was. *And is!* she thought.

In the Deep South, when a big thunderstorm was imminent, farmers—seeming to always be in need of rain—had a common expression, "I think it's coming up a cloud!" It was an *exciting* event for them most of the time.

Lou Ellen and Burt went to visit her daddy and mother one hot August weekend after they had permanently moved into the house with Granny Simpson. Granny had passed away by then. Her apartment across the hall was unoccupied, and she and Burt stayed there when they visited.

The house was not air conditioned, so Burt opened the windows and wooden door and latched the screen door, inviting any hint of a cool breeze that might waft by. A fan sat in the floor and hummed on high speed, though it merely stirred the humidity. They had barely dozed off when numerous lightning bolts spider webbed the sky, lighting up their bedroom and the world outside.

Without further warning, the storm announced itself with a sky-splitting boom of thunder so forceful the windows rattled, making the whole house seem to quake. It had hardly finished its rumble before the next one boomed and somersaulted across the sky. The wind rose and began to deliver sheets of rain. They both had woken up, probably *before* the first wake-the-dead reverberation, but neither knew for sure the other was awake. For a couple of minutes, neither of them spoke. Then Burt apparently couldn't restrain himself any longer. With feigned fear, he placed a shaky hand on her shoulder.

"I th-think … it's … c-coming up … a c-cloud!" he whispered in a frightened child's voice. Lou Ellen burst into peals of laughter, and Burt joined in as they welcomed the cooling breeze and enjoyed the sound of the rain on the rooftop.

One night Lou Ellen was in the kitchen cooking and started to tell Burt something while he was watching television in the adjoining den, but she could see he was more interested in the pretty girl on the screen than he was in her story. So she stopped talking. A few seconds later, he realized what he was doing.

"Okay, I'm listening now. What were you trying to tell me?" he said, as he walked around the breakfast bar into the kitchen.

"Too late! I'm not going to tell you now," she replied. "Go back to your television show."

"Oh! Please, tell me, honey. I'm sorry I wasn't paying attention before," he begged, beginning to dramatize.

"Nope … too late now," she said, turning back to the sink.

"Oh, no! I *have* to know what it was. It'll drive me *crazy* if you don't tell me … *please* tell me."

"Nope!" she spoke with finality.

This called for begging on his knees, and she knew Burt had no qualms about doing so when he was in his clown mode. When that failed to get results, he resorted to more extreme measures. He got down in the floor and played the "dead cockroach" scene, lying on his back with arms and feet pawing the air, begging her to tell him. Of course by then Lou Ellen was laughing so hard she had forgotten what she wanted to tell him anyway, but she didn't confess.

"No, I'm not telling you now," she kept repeating until he finally gave up. Years later he still mentioned how much he hated he missed that story!

"Since you *still* won't tell me, I'll probably go to my grave, never knowing what good story I missed!" he said.

Probably! Unless by some miracle I remember what it was! she thought, smiling.

On Sundays Lou Ellen always laid out Burt's suit or sports coat and pants, shirt, tie, and socks because he couldn't match colors and hated making decisions, especially about clothes. Unless she selected for him, he would choose the same outfit over and over. One Sunday morning after she'd put his clothes out, she was sitting at her vanity when he came and stood in her bathroom doorway.

"Does this outfit look okay to you?" he asked.

She looked up and immediately burst out laughing. He was dressed from top to bottom in shirt, tie, sports coat, underwear, socks, and shoes ... with no pants on! She had forgotten to lay out his pants. Lou Ellen thought the hilarity of that scene was rivaled only by the "knobby knees" Geraldine character.

Burt loved to scare Lou Ellen and was always teasing and pestering her. She was too old to bite, so she took up hurling objects—anything close enough to reach. Burt said he had learned early to run as fast as he could as soon as he did something to her, and even that failed to save him sometimes. He declared she could throw water through a keyhole, and that he'd learned he should never bother her when she had her hands in water or had a glass of tea or cup of coffee—unless he was prepared to run. And he admitted he just couldn't resist the temptation most of the time. Sometimes there was a big mess to clean up afterward; but they both thought it was well worth it in fun and laughter.

Now she smiled, remembering the morning she'd been brushing her teeth in the bathroom and had thought of something she wanted to tell Burt. Thinking he was still sitting at the breakfast table reading the paper, with toothbrush in hand, she walked out the door to tell him. Burt was lurking just outside the door. As she appeared, he grabbed her.

"Boo!" he growled loudly, immediately taking flight down the hall toward the kitchen.

She threw her toothbrush at him; he picked it up, tossed it into the garbage can as he passed by, and kept on running!

All these years later when they laughed about things they'd done, Burt told her he couldn't remember how, but he was sure she got even. According to him, she always did! He said he'd learned early in their marriage that those mischievous things he couldn't resist doing might have retributions that could be hazardous to his health and well-being. But he said he just couldn't help it—the little imp in him just wouldn't behave.

We've had such a blessed, fun-filled life together, she thought.

Most of the time Lou Ellen couldn't outwit Burt, but there were a few times when she felt she had gotten even. One occasion came to her mind in particular, which had occurred when he wasn't feeling well.

"I don't feel real *bad*—just not quite up to par today," Burt said.

"Do you feel feverish?" she asked.

"No, not really…I just feel…a little *puny.*"

"Well, just to be on the safe side, let's check your temperature!" she said as she went to the medicine cabinet for the thermometer.

"Here you go, sweetie," she said as she put the thermometer under his tongue and waited the required time.

Taking the thermometer out of his mouth, she kissed his forehead and said, "Okay, let's see if you are sick or if you just need some TLC."

She held it up to the light to read, and with a shocked, apologetic voice she said, "Oh! My gosh! Burt, I am *sooo* sorry! I accidentally used the *rectal* thermometer!"

The incredulous look on his face was priceless. If only she'd had a camera! Of course Lou Ellen started laughing hysterically, and Burt thought it was pretty funny too, *after* he realized he'd been had.

As with any marriage, Lou Ellen and Burt had definitely had peaks and valleys, but she knew God had always sustained them. She and Burt didn't have one of those "never had an argument" marriages either. *How boring!* she thought.

They were total opposites in so many ways. He was slow and meticulous; she was fast and full-throttle, almost to the point of being accident-prone sometimes. He was messy—organization was not in his vocabulary—and he could be the all-time procrastinator winner. By comparison to *him,* she was the neat nick, *mostly* organized, and procrastinated only a little; however, she was impatient to a fault, and too much of a perfectionist wannabe. Adding fuel to the fire, they were both quick tempered. To put it mildly, they had some pretty lively conversations, but an hour later the arguments were forgotten. Most of the time they didn't even remember what had actually started them. In their early marriage, Burt always won the arguments by teasing and acting the buffoon until she laughed. *Who can stay mad when they are laughing?*

Burt's constant and sometimes goofy sense of humor had sustained Lou Ellen through many difficult and tense situations as well, particularly with her daddy and mother. He had a special gift. He could joke and tease to ease the tension, and he could find humor in practically every situation.

Lou Ellen felt Burt's generosity with her was equally unselfish and boundless. Since she had known him, there was nothing she could ask for that he would not get for her, even if it meant going into debt to get it. Luckily she had always been responsible enough to ask within reason, or they might have ended up in the poorhouse.

Lou Ellen always knew that God's love was unconditional. When Burt entered her life, she came to realize his love for her was unconditional too. Through example, he taught her how to express her love, to laugh, and to enjoy life.

Lou Ellen often remembered the day when Burt's mom was alive, and she and Mom had been talking about their childhoods. She had told Mom about her own need as a child to know somebody, somewhere loved her.

"Well, you don't have to worry about lack of love *anymore,* do you?" Mom said.

"No, I don't, but I just don't understand why some people from the same economic and cultural background, and even of the same generation, can be so different. For example, my parents versus you and Dad. You two had a rough life too, but you love deeply. There is never a question about that. You *show* it. You hug, and you say, 'I love you' all the time."

"I wish I knew the answer, Lou Ellen, but I know things are not always the way they seem. I guess we'd just have to know the whole story of a person's background and what may or may not have happened in his or her life to make them the way they are."

"I understand that too, but then there's another side of the coin ... like Mr. Worthington. If you listen to him talk about the good old days, it sounds like he was born with the proverbial silver spoon ... he had perfect parents, plenty of money, a college education, and on and on ... but he doesn't *act* like a loving man. With that frown always etched on his face, he just seems to me to be an unhappy person. He's just an old curmudgeon, and I have a hard time picturing him loving anyone—or for that matter *being* loved," Lou Ellen said, her voice taking a new tone and fire beginning to flicker in her eyes.

Smiling at Lou Ellen's tirade, Mom said, "I think he's just—"

"And I don't know how his wife puts up with him! I'd tell him to shape up or ship out!" Lou Ellen spat, as Mom laughed out loud.

"Yes, he's a real card all right, but some people put on a false front for some unknown reason. Some people love, but you might never know they do, or how deeply."

"Mom, that may be true for *some,* but Burt's eyes are the windows to his soul. He loves so deeply you can almost see it oozing from his pores; love *shows* on Burt! I can feel it and see it."

"That's for sure, Lou Ellen. Burt loves you so much that when he looks at you, it looks to me like he could eat you with a spoon!"

Lou Ellen laughed, but she knew it was true. And she knew he loved his family with equal depth. When she and Burt met and fell in love, she no longer had that deep-seated incessant need to make other people approve of her, accept, and love her. She had Burt, and she didn't need another human being. His love was all she needed. She was free to be her own person, with her own opinions, needs, and desires … free to pursue her goals and accomplish them. Burt gave her complete freedom to be herself. She smiled, remembering a conversation they'd once had about her independent nature.

"Yeah! Sure! You just took over. You became my boss!" Burt said to her, his eyes squinting with mischief.

"Well, *you* robbed the cradle. *You* raised me; so it's entirely *your* fault how I turned out—good or bad!" she retorted.

"No … you were already mean when I got you! I've struggled just to survive!" he said, trying to suppress the smile puckering his mouth.

"Malarkey! But I hope you have your affairs in order because you're a dead man walking! No! Correction … you're a dead man running!" she said as she chased him out the back door and around the house, both of them laughing. They'd had many such bantering good times.

Through all their years together, she had always known that Burt was on her side. He was her staunch supporter—always there for her, no matter what. Even if he didn't always totally agree, he respected her right to her own opinion, and he was right there in her corner to support and comfort her. She could depend on him one hundred and ten percent!

Additionally, Burt was Lou Ellen's greatest encourager. She felt he had never had a doubt that she was capable of doing whatever she wanted or set out to do. Sometimes she thought he'd always had more faith in her than she had in herself.

Burt had always been the wind beneath her wings.

CHAPTER TWENTY-TWO

While sitting on the patio having their morning coffee and listening to the birds singing, Burt and Lou Ellen laughed and talked about the humorous clips they'd seen on one of the funny home video shows on television the night before. The animal ones were Lou Ellen's favorites.

Burt finished his coffee and left to go out and work in his garden, but she re-filled her cup and went back out. She planned to work in her flower beds a bit and enjoy the cool morning. She sat down to finish her coffee and started thinking about the pets they'd had through the years and how much fun they'd had with them. And she thought about her daddy and how he'd loved to laugh and how much he had seemed to enjoy coming to visit them when he was still living. He'd enjoyed their pets too.

When his mental health was good, Lou Ellen's daddy loved life, loved people, loved to laugh, and was a real practical joker. Once when she and Burt went to visit them, her daddy tied a knot at the bottom of both of Burt's pant legs while they were sleeping one night. The next morning when Burt woke up and tried to put them on, he knew immediately who the perpetrator was, and her daddy laughed heartily when he accused him.

Later that same day Burt and Daniel were outside in his garden doing some small gardening chores, and fire ants crawled up inside Burt's pant legs—biting *everywhere!* With lightning speed he discarded his shoes, socks, *and* pants right there on the spot while her daddy doubled over laughing. And for as long as he lived, her daddy continued to tease Burt about taking his pants off outside for everybody to see.

When Daniel was well, he came to spend a month with Lou Ellen and the family every year, but Lena always stayed with Granny Simpson. He made several trips to visit them while they lived in Colorado Springs, going by bus until Lou Ellen convinced him flying was much faster. He really liked flying, and from then on, she always sent him a plane ticket.

She never heard her daddy say a curse word worse than "*ding*," which he said often. One December he flew to Colorado Springs for the month so he could spend Christmas with them. Every day he took a walk to the convenience store nearby and asked his youngest grandson, Ryan, to walk with him. One evening they had a big snowstorm, and it turned brutally cold afterward. The next morning it was beautiful and sunny, and Pike's Peak glistened through their front picture window; but it was actually hovering at zero degrees outside. Opening the door to get a better look outside, Lou Ellen thought it appeared as though someone had thrown a blanket of wool over the whole city—breathtakingly beautiful. She called her daddy to come see.

"Daddy, have you ever seen anything more amazing?" she asked.

"I never thought I'd see so much snow. It's real purty."

Soon she saw her daddy begin to put his coat on.

"Daddy, you really shouldn't go out this morning," she said. "It looks nice and warm with the sun shining, but it's much too cold to go for a walk since you don't have the proper clothes for this kind of weather."

"Nah! I'll be fine … my jacket'll be enough, and we won't be gone long."

Lou Ellen tried again to discourage it, but to no avail. He called Ryan to tell him it was time for their walk, and he put his jacket on. Since they lived there, they all had plenty of warm clothes, including the snowmobile suit and felt lined boots that

Ryan donned. Her daddy wore a larger size jacket than Burt, so she couldn't help him out in that department, but she gave him a pair of Burt's gloves. A few minutes later, Ryan and his Papa set out up the cold, slippery sidewalk.

Approximately five minutes later, her daddy came huffing and puffing back through the door.

"Ding! My yurs got too cold!" he said, rubbing his ears.

Sometimes experience is the best teacher, even for the aged! Lou Ellen thought.

Lou Ellen had a spoiled black toy poodle she'd named Prissy, who had an automatically scheduled appointment with the pet groomer every six weeks. Lou Ellen didn't go regularly to the beauty shop, but the dog did! Prissy always had either hot pink or bright red bows on her ears, with nail polish to match, and she looked adorable. Many people of her daddy's generation, especially those who lived in the country, were of the opinion that dogs and cats lived outside, never inside the house. They certainly could not understand pampering them to the extent Prissy was. So Lou Ellen could never get her daddy to say Prissy was cute. He would only say, "She's got cute *ways!*" But she always knew her daddy loved and enjoyed Prissy far more than he would admit.

Once when her daddy was visiting for a month, he tied Prissy's long ears on top of her head and was thoroughly amused with the results. She did look rather cute and comical and didn't seem to mind. She loved being played with in any fashion, and she always begged for a bite of anything they were eating. While her daddy was eating an orange one day, Prissy kept begging him for some. Her daddy took a piece of the orange peel between his thumb and forefinger, held it down to her and squeezed it, thinking she would not like the taste. Instead, some of the acid got into her eyes; so she put her face down into the carpet and repeatedly rubbed it back and forth … to her daddy's great mirth. From that day on, for as long as she lived, when Daniel came to visit and merely held his empty thumb and forefinger down as though offering Prissy something to eat, she would immediately repeat the face in the carpet routine. Her daddy would laugh uproariously every time, and Prissy kept him entertained with that and many more of her similar cute antics.

Another lesson Prissy never forgot also involved food. Since she loved spaghetti, at dinner one night Lou Ellen put some spaghetti in her food bowl, which she had not first allowed to cool to an edible temperature. Prissy immediately took a bite, jumped back and sat staring at it for a little while before she finally ate it. From that day on, any time Lou Ellen gave her spaghetti—even *cold* spaghetti—she sat in front of it and watched and waited until *she* deemed it cool enough to eat.

When they lived in their two-story home with a full basement in Colorado, Kevin and Ryan took their snacks downstairs to the den. They played a game with Prissy whereby they deliberately wouldn't share their snacks with her—just to get her to go upstairs to find Lou Ellen and "tattle" on them. Prissy would find Lou Ellen, run toward the stairs and back to her, repeating the routine until Lou Ellen followed her down the stairs. Prissy then ran to the kids and watched her as she approached and pretended to spank Kevin and Ryan on the leg.

"You give that baby a bite!" She would say to them, and at that point, they shared with Prissy. Lou Ellen went back upstairs, and the boys repeated the routine again. The three of them loved to play that game with Prissy, repeating it numerous times until Lou Ellen, exhausted from running up and down the stairs, called it quits.

CHAPTER
TWENTY-THREE

The noise sounded like a phone ringing, but it seemed so far away...like it was buried someplace. Slowly it dawned on her...it wasn't far away. It was right next to her bed. Lou Ellen opened her eyes to thin slits and noticed Burt's side of the bed was empty. Picking up the phone, she tried to speak into the wrong end, quickly reversed it, and croaked, "H-hello."

"Well, it's about time you answered that phone. Why in the world are you still sleeping at this hour? It's seven in the morning, for crying out loud!" her friend Roselyn said in her usual teasing manner.

Lou Ellen looked at the clock and saw it was only six. "For *you* maybe; you're an hour ahead of me. Remember?"

"Of course I remember, but if I have to be up, you might as well be too," she said, laughing. "Anyway...Happy Birthday!"

Lou Ellen groaned. "You silly goose, it's at least two months or more until my birthday."

"I know that, but we're going on a cruise then, and I won't be here," Roselyn said, laughing. "I really called because we haven't talked in ages, and I've missed that," she added.

They laughed and talked for nearly an hour, promised to get together soon, and hung up.

Lou Ellen couldn't remember where she heard it said that friends are the flowers in the garden of life, but it was so true for her. She believed friends were forever. Sometimes they come, sometimes they go, but they still leave a profound and lasting effect for a lifetime.

Roselyn and Lou Ellen had been good friends since they'd all lived in Colorado Springs and then in Florida. Roselyn and her husband, Randy, lived in North Carolina now, but they'd often reminisced and enjoyed the good memories of those days together all over again. They e-mailed often and visited each other too, though not often enough.

One morning the four of them went out to breakfast, along with a couple who were friends of Roselyn and Randy. After they ate, Lou Ellen and the others sauntered out across the parking lot toward the car while Burt was paying the bill. As they neared the vehicle, Burt suddenly came running out the restaurant door, stumbling, arms outstretched, yelling, "Don't leave me, don't leave me," in a loud and pitiful, childish voice. Everyone in the entire parking lot turned to see what all the brouhaha was about.

"Oh, it's just that goofy Burt. Y'all...let's hurry to the car before anybody associates him with us!" Randy said.

Laughing, they all ran, got into the car, and locked the doors. But Burt made an even worse commotion from the outside looking in, so they eventually had to claim him to keep him quiet.

Lou Ellen invited Roselyn and Randy to dinner one night. After dessert they retired to the living room, where they sat quietly talking and listening to music. Burt was sitting in an easy chair, Indian-style, with legs crossed and feet underneath him. Suddenly, he let out the most forceful humongous sneeze. As he did, he catapulted himself, with seemingly effortless motion, straight from the chair onto the floor—with not one inch of change to his sitting position. How he did it, not even he could later explain; but it was such a hilarious sight that, at one point, Lou Ellen thought they might have to resuscitate Roselyn.

Like Burt, Randy was equally fun loving and witty. The four of them went to the Sanford Flea Market one Saturday, where there were practically wall-to-wall people milling through the maze of wings and aisles so complex it was easy to get temporarily lost from each other. For unknown reasons, Burt and Randy started acting goofy—being their *usual* selves, actually. Burt pretended to be reprimanding Randy, as though Randy was his son.

"Now, you'd better not go running off and get lost from us," he said as he pointed his finger in Randy's face.

Not to be outdone and playing along, Randy went around behind Burt, put his index and middle fingers into both Burt's back pockets, and shuffled along behind him, pretending to be a little child.

"Daddy told me to do dis. He said I might get waust," Randy said to people they passed, repeating it over and over as they walked down the aisles. People began staring and pointing, and Lou Ellen and Roselyn dissolved in laughter. Lou Ellen was sure people were wondering what could possibly be wrong with those weird adults.

"Don't worry. We will be taking them back home before five o'clock," Roselyn began telling people.

"Yeah … five p.m. That's their curfew!" Lou Ellen would add as she and Roselyn got even more tickled.

It was one of the few times Lou Ellen saw Burt get embarrassed. Finally he got free and purposely got *himself* lost from *Randy*. Sometimes the two of them surprised even Roselyn and her with their numerous and varied outrageous antics, and they had a lot of fun together.

Lou Ellen thought of Jeremy and Sue and what a blessing they had been throughout the years. They'd had a long and memorable relationship, still lived close, and they visited as often as their busy schedules allowed. They had two sons just as Burt and Lou Ellen did. The eldest was born in the same year and month as Kevin, and their youngest in the same year as Ryan, only a month apart. Jeremy and Sue would always be in the good memories of her past—and present.

At eight o'clock, Burt opened the bedroom door, carrying a bag from McDonald's that brought a tantalizing aroma into the bedroom. Seeing her up and putting her robe on, he starting singing, "Good morning to you, good—"

"Burt, you're in trouble! Don't you remember the seven o'clock rule?"

"Of course I do! I had an errand to run early this morning. That's why I let you sleep late. But look…you get breakfast in bed…and you get to share it with a handsome man!" Burt said, grinning like a Cheshire cat.

"Then where's the *man?*" she said, looking all around the room while trying to keep a straight face.

"Ooh, you really know how to hurt a guy! I'm crushed!" he groaned.

"Hah! Seriously, food sounds great to me. I'm hungry! I've been awake since Roselyn woke me up…at *six!* She got even. The last time we talked, I called her late at night."

"You two have *always* had fun pulling pranks on each other. All right…we'll eat, but first things first," he said, as he gathered her into his arms for a big hug and kiss.

CHAPTER TWENTY-FOUR

Lou Ellen went to bed earlier than usual that night. At one a.m. she was awakened by some wild animals making noises out near the shelter where she fed her cats. *It must be raccoons getting into a fuss over the cat food,* she thought. She couldn't get back to sleep, and she didn't want to wake Burt. She eased out of bed and went to the guest room to read for a while. But she couldn't get interested in the book. Her mind kept wandering. She stared at the ceiling and watched as the good memories of the past with her family seemed to swirl around in her head like a carousel.

While living in Colorado Springs, the Newmans' favorite pastime was going camping in the Rocky Mountains or the foothills of the Rockies.

They'd had only one *tent* camping experience in the Rockies, and that was enough for Lou Ellen. She knew there were bears in the Rockies, and that night she'd heard bears in the garbage can outside their tent. Burt told her it was raccoons, but she knew raccoons couldn't make such loud smacking noises. A week later they went RV camper shopping, but Burt always teased her about her "big smacker" bear.

Sometimes when they went camping, it might be ninety-five degrees when they left Colorado Springs; but when they got to their campsite, they had beautiful warm days and chilly nights, resulting in comfort-plus sleeping conditions. She remembered one camping trip when they'd camped at a slightly higher altitude than usual. It turned cold during the night, and they awoke the next morning to find frost scattered like ashes over the campsite. But it had quickly disappeared shortly after sunrise.

Simply driving along the highways cut through huge mountains and looking up to see gigantic overhanging boulders had been awe inspiring. Occasionally a boulder made big news when it slid down the side of the mountain and crashed into the highway, sometimes snarling traffic for hours. They loved the historical areas such as Leadville, where they toured the old silver mining areas and the cabin where Horace Tabor, known as The Silver King, and Baby Doe had once lived.

Of all the beauty of Colorado, Lou Ellen's favorite was the scenery on the drive across Trail Ridge Road: over fifty miles of the highest continuous motorway in the United States, with a maximum elevation of over twelve thousand feet. Spectacular views of breathtaking scenery left her speechless, regardless of the number of times they drove across. Seeing the majestic Rocky Mountains was awesome enough, but far down below she gazed in wonder at the golden shimmering aspen trees clustered among all the dark green evergreens. Deep blue lakes nestled throughout, and swiftly flowing mountain streams snaked around or over boulders and between the trees.

Because so much snow fell at the top along the trail, it was only open for travel during the summer for a couple of months. It sometimes had snow during the open season also, which resulted in a temporary closure. Lou Ellen always prayed they wouldn't need snow chains before they made it across the ridge. She didn't relish the idea of sliding down the side of one of those switchback mountain roads into one of the bodies of water below, beautiful though they were! They often stopped at many of the scenic overlooks and always stopped at the Continental Divide for pictures. Burt told the boys they could pour water on the west side and it would end up in the Pacific Ocean, or they could pour water on the east side and it would end up in the Atlantic Ocean.

When Kevin and Ryan were young teenagers, Burt and Lou Ellen took them to the Heritage Square Opera House, a well-known dinner playhouse in the foothills of the mountains, where they had reserved balcony seats to see a popular melodrama. As they usually did after the play, the cast performed an hour-long olio of comedy skits, jokes, music solos, etc. During one of the skits, the entire auditorium was darkened. A single spotlight beamed down to the center of the stage, where one of the lady cast members stood. She pretended she was doing a séance.

"Ar-r-thur?" she called through the microphone in a soft but long, drawn-out voice. It was pin-dropping-quiet.

"Ar-r-thur?" Still, all was quiet. And the third time she called for Arthur's spirit, though not scripted, a loud voice from the balcony yelled out.

"Wha-at?"

Who else but Burt would even consider such a stunt?

The actress was momentarily stymied. Then she got so tickled she had trouble finishing her skit. Both Kevin and Ryan laughed out loud while trying to dissolve into their seats. They may have been just a tad embarrassed at the time, but later they admitted they thought it was really funny.

CHAPTER TWENTY-FIVE

Both Kevin and Ryan inherited Burt's sense of humor. After they grew up, had families of their own and came home to visit, they usually tried to coordinate schedules to arrive the same week. It always resulted in the most enjoyable, hilarious week of fun and laughter for all. When putting three comics together, each trying to outdo the other, Lou Ellen knew she had to be prepared to laugh until she had trouble breathing and her ribs and stomach hurt. The second day was even worse.

Some of their most memorable family times had occurred around the dinner table. They'd had many fun discussions about how Lou Ellen had disciplined Kevin and Ryan with her eyes when they were kids, and each of them tried to tell embellished childhood tales taller than his brother's. But they both said they knew when they'd best stop whatever they were doing and behave themselves when they were growing up, simply by looking at her eyes.

Lou Ellen had always been prone to call both Kevin and Ryan by the other's name, so it was not at all unusual to them. They just rolled their eyes, smiled at each other, corrected her, and the conversation continued. But one night at the dinner table while looking at Ryan, she said, "Kevin, would you please pass me the butter?"

Always quick with a comeback, Ryan replied, "Sure, here you are *Dad!*" His brother exuberantly congratulated him, slapped him on the back, and they laughed and enjoyed the moment.

Cheeky, like father, like son … smart aleck comedians! Lou Ellen thought, smiling. *You two will pay! I will put you in the kitchen washing pots and pans after dinner.* She imagined she could hear them begging already. Even a dead cockroach routine wouldn't help *them* out either! She could hardly keep from laughing out loud just thinking about what their reactions would be.

And pots and pans they did wash! She took pictures for posterity. When showing them the pictures a few years later, they whispered to each other and looked at her with the impish demeanor that was always palpable when they were together.

"Yeah, Mom…we remember…that was the day you mistreated us and made us wash pots and pans," Kevin said.

"While we were on vacation, no less!" Ryan added.

"Poor babies!" Lou Ellen mocked.

Kevin and Ryan often teamed up to tease her. Usually when she was frying cornbread, she had to fry a platter stacked high with thin, crusty pieces approximately three inches in diameter. They took turns distracting her while the other stole two pieces of bread from the platter and ran outside, and they enjoyed it even more when she chased them with the wooden spoon. If she freely offered them a piece of bread from the platter, they'd decline.

"No, Mom, it just doesn't taste as good as the ones we snitch!" Kevin said, causing Burt to chuckle. *The apple doesn't fall far from the tree,* she thought.

"I don't know how I've survived the three of you clowns all these years," she said, truthfully enjoying every moment of their mischief. But Ryan never let her get the last word.

"Oh! Huh! Cry me a river… *I'm* still going to a therapist after all these years, because I was so traumatized by your mean eyes when I was a kid. The shrink says I may be *permanently* damaged!" he quipped as he jerked his head repeatedly, pretending he had a tic. He and his brother guffawed, gave each other high fives, and continued their tomfoolery.

"If you two don't get out of here, I am going to make sure you are *both* permanently damaged; you won't *need* therapy. It will be useless!" Lou Ellen said, as she chased them out of the kitchen while they yelled for help and ran, laughing. All she had to do was threaten to find them a dishwashing job, and she wouldn't see them again until she announced dinner. But she enjoyed them too much.

Lou Ellen often remembered a family vacation that was not particularly funny to her at the time, but in retrospect had been quite comical and definitely unforgettable. Everyone else thought it was the best vacation ever! But she called it "our vacation to Camp Flood World." She had written it all down in her journal to assure that she would always remember it in detail, in case she ever became senile and entertained the thought of going tent camping with her family again. *Not!*

Burt and Lou Ellen were living in Cape Canaveral, Florida; Kevin and his family were living in Merritt Island, Florida; and Ryan and his family were living in San Antonio, Texas. She and Burt had a total of five grandchildren, ranging in ages between four and twelve. They planned a family camping trip to Valley Lake—to this exact place where she and Burt now lived. But at the time it was just property four hundred miles away, which they'd invested in for retirement purposes. Retiring and building a dream home were still just that: dreams. It was in the same city where their friends, Jeremy and Sue, lived at the time.

It was the month of June, perfect for camping and ideal for the grandkids, because the property consisted of twelve acres with two ponds of catfish, bass, and brim. It had two tall security lights, was fenced, and had a locking gate. The camping area was a large, slightly sloped grassy area between the two ponds, formerly a cow pasture. At the bottom of the slope among the shade trees, they had placed a small motor home that slept two people—Burt and Lou Ellen—plus one cute little dog! The property also had an abundance of mosquitoes, two or more destructive beavers, and heaven only knew how many poisonous snakes, bullfrogs, and other critters. Kevin and Ryan loved to snake and beaver hunt and were anticipating having more fun than the kids.

They all coordinated the dates, organized everything perfectly, and assigned each family the different camping gear they were in charge of. According to the plans, Kevin and his wife, Sandi, and their two children were scheduled to arrive on Friday, and Ryan and his wife, Ashley, and their three children would be arriving on Saturday. There would be a total of twelve people because Kevin's young sister-in-law, Patti, was going to vacation with them. Kevin, Ryan, and the three grandsons, Noah, Jacob, and Evan, were planning to tent camp. Lou Ellen had rented a large motor home at a campground a couple of miles away where Sandi, Ashley, Patti, and the two granddaughters, Jennifer and Stephanie, were going to sleep. Everyone was so looking forward to that vacation and could hardly wait for the day to come.

On Thursday, Burt and Lou Ellen left Cape Canaveral with their vehicle loaded down much like the Clampetts of the *Beverly Hillbillies* going to Hollywood. They were going a day early to get things set up, mow the grass, get a port-a-potty to put on the site, set up the awning, etc. They had bought a new riding lawn mower and left it there only four weeks earlier. They had thought of everything!

They arrived safely only to discover they had left the key to unlock the gate into the property in Cape Canaveral! Not to worry. They remembered they had given Jeremy and Sue a key, so they went to Jeremy's house, only to find nobody home. Lucky for them, Sue had left a window slightly open for her cats, so Lou Ellen raised the window, went inside, stole their property key, and went back to unlock the gate. And all would have been fine, except the electric power company had also put one of *their* locks on the gate for meter-reading purposes, and Burt and Lou Ellen didn't have a key for it.

No problem. They drove to the convenience store a mile away to use the payphone to call the power company and have them drive out and open the gate. Someone was using the payphone, so Burt waited … and waited … it seemed an hour. Time was of the essence; the power company would be closing in ten minutes. He gave up and drove to the power company's office. They arrived just minutes before the office closed for the day, and they obtained a key at last.

They were over hurdle one!

First on the agenda was to mow the knee-high grass with the new, bright red riding mower.

"Honey, could you get me the key to the mower?" Burt asked.

"What key? I don't have the key, Burt."

"Oh man! Don't tell me we left that key in Florida too!

"*Oops*...it's probably hanging right beside the property key in Cape Canaveral!"

On Friday, Kevin and family arrived from Florida with the camping tent and equipment. So did the rain showers! Wanting to be a good grandma, between showers Lou Ellen waded into the pond edges with the grandkids to gather tadpoles and minnows, where something—possibly a spider—bit her on the ankle. It was swollen, sore, and painful the entire week.

Burt's truck, which usually stayed on the property, had mechanical problems, so it had to be put in the garage; therefore, Burt had to rent a trailer in order to go to the next town to rent and haul the port-a-potty to the campsite, using Lou Ellen's car.

They were over hurdle two.

And they had a stroke of luck. Through the local lawn mower dealer, Burt managed to get a key for the lawn mower and was able to get the grass cut.

Whew! They were over hurdle three!

On Saturday, along with the rain, Ryan and family arrived from Texas with the portable screen room he had borrowed to bring with him, just in case the mosquitoes tried to carry everyone away. Between rain showers, the men took it out and started to erect it … no luck there … it was missing a major part!

They simply forgot about that hurdle! It was their unwritten rule: when camping, make do!

Late that Saturday night, Kevin and Ryan's boys went to bed in the tent, their wives and daughters left for the campground motor home, and Burt and Lou Ellen went to bed in their motor home. But Kevin and Ryan had just been waiting until all the kids went to bed so they could go fishing in the small aluminum boat, just the two of them.

Sunday morning at breakfast, Kevin and Ryan had everyone's undivided attention.

"Y'all won't believe the experience we had after y'all went to bed," Kevin said.

All eyes were on him, and the kids got excited, begging him to hurry up and tell them what happened.

"We hung a huge fish about two a.m.—," Ryan began.

"Uh-oh … everybody pick your feet up … it's about to get deep around here!" Lou Ellen interrupted.

"Yep … a fantastic, *big* fish story is about to unfold!" Burt joined in.

"I told you that you wouldn't believe it, but it's true. He pulled us all over the pond in that lightweight boat!" Kevin said.

"*How* big, Daddy?" Noah wanted to know.

"What kind of fish, Daddy?" Jacob asked.

"Where is it?" four-year-old Evan asked, his eyes big with excitement.

"Yeah! Let's go see it," Stephanie said as she and Jennifer jumped up to go.

"We don't know what kind it was. It could've been a catfish or a big bass—," Ryan started to explain.

"What happened to it?" Noah interrupted.

"Well, it finally got off the hook ... we lost it!" Ryan said.

"Oh, *Dad!* That's a joke for sure," Noah said as he and all the other kids started laughing and teasing them.

"Uncle Ryan, you don't expect us to believe that, do you?" Jennifer asked.

"Kevin, you were right; nobody believes us. We should have just kept it *our* big fish secret."

"Well, if you don't have proof—not even a scale or two—you'll have to admit it does seem to be just a great ... but unbelievable ... fish story!" Lou Ellen told them. "It sounds about as likely as my ability to sell oceanfront property in downtown Phoenix!"

Considering their penchant for besting each other, Burt hadn't been willing to bet on the truth of that fish tale either. But that was their story, and they stuck to it!

On Sunday it rained and rained without ceasing. Burt and Lou Ellen had taken a sun canopy, a small TV/VCR, lawn chairs, and cartoon videos for the kids to watch. They had erected the canopy on Thursday, and they had even thought to take a tarp to throw over the canopy in case it rained. In case it rained? It did not *stop* raining! Pretty soon the tarp filled with water, sank in the middle, and fell in! Or was that the awning on the motor home? She lost track. It rained so much that water came gushing down the slope under the motor home, taking camping gear and other miscellany with it. So the men had to dig a moat around the motor home to divert the water.

Were they having fun yet?

The kids all fished in the rain, and with the grown-ups' help, all caught fish. *They* had fun at least. By night time on Sunday, the tents were water-logged, leaking—pouring, actually—so the five guys abandoned it and joined the girls. All ten of them slept in the motor home in the campground, which Lou Ellen had been told *could* sleep ten, compactly of course.

Blue Monday dawned with more rain. They teased the kids about gathering the animals by twos and told Noah to make sure his ark was rainproof and unsinkable. It was rather entertaining just listening to Kevin and Ryan's descriptions of ten of them sleeping in the motor home ... of the sleeping positions they had to assume, stories of kids talking in their sleep, and numerous other tall tales and complaints!

"The tent is still available if y'all would rather have it," Burt quipped.

They were no longer able to drive the cars inside the gate, so they parked out along the paved street and walked in. The women went to the store and bought the kids a "splish-splash" waterslide toy. It didn't work!

"Too much water for it," Ryan said wryly.

Tuesday, rain had a companion ... the wind. It blew, it rained, and blew and rained some more. Noah caught a seven-and-a-half-pound catfish and was beyond thrilled. He didn't even know it was raining.

"Oh, that fish doesn't even compare to the lunker that pulled us around in the boat," his daddy told him.

"But, Dad, you and Uncle Kevin don't have a scale of proof ... remember? Yours doesn't count. Hurry, PaPa, take a picture of mine! I need proof!" Noah told Burt.

Wednesday morning they awoke to a glorious sight...the sun! But by the time it reached ninety-four degrees, all the moisture made a perfect sauna. The mosquitoes and gnats loved it, but the Newman clan was miserable.

They were scheduled to go to Cloverton to Burt's Aunt Willie's house for lunch, and the "honey wagon" was supposed to come to the property to empty the port-a-potty. To say it needed to be emptied *badly* was an understatement. Burt left the honey wagon employee a note instructing him to open the gate and go ahead and service it if they weren't back.

That afternoon when they arrived back at the campsite, the serviceman had left Burt a note saying that the ground was too boggy. He couldn't get in with his heavy equipment to service it, but he said he would come back Friday! Lou Ellen thought he just had to be pulling a cruel joke, and she was vocal about it. She should not have complained. The rain came back, and the mosquitoes loved them.

Thursday was the only day they didn't have rain, but they had another sweltering steam bath day of ninety-four degrees. They had a campfire that night to deter the mosquitoes, which were even worse at nighttime, and they made scrumptious homemade ice cream to celebrate the dry weather. But they mostly wanted to cool down!

Friday afternoon brought more rain! They waited for the honey wagon to arrive to service the port-a-potty as the employee's note had indicated, but it didn't come! The girls were not thrilled about using it when it was fresh and clean; by Friday they debated about going in there at all! They *all* debated!

Lou Ellen was sick and tired of preparing food for twelve people for a week, in the rain, under the tiny awning of a small motor home. Everyone's favorite food, fried cornbread, was not fun to fry with the hot grease popping everywhere because of frequent, errant raindrops. So she gave up cooking, and they all went out to dinner.

That night it stopped raining, and they had a campfire, pudgy pies, and s'mores... along with some ghost stories and other questionable tales that kept the kids entertained.

Saturday morning the Texas gang left, and Burt and Kevin very carefully loaded the port-a-potty on the back of the truck and took it back to the rental business... filled to capacity! In fact they drove rather slowly to avoid even a chance that it might tip slightly. Of course they could make anything humorous.

"I know what we should do, Mom," Kevin said. "I'll prop the door open, write *Kevin for President* on it, and sit on the seat while Dad drives down the highway! What do you think?"

"I think, Kevin, that you'd be a shoo-in—"

"You think I'd win, do you?"

"You would! But it'd be Redneck Man of the Year," Lou Ellen said, chuckling.

"Well... second place is not worth it. I'll forget that idea."

Burt, Lou Ellen, and Kevin spent the entire afternoon washing up, cleaning up a week's worth of trash for twelve people, putting away fishing poles and gear, cleaning the motor home, packing up, and loading up the vehicle for the trip back home the next morning.

Everybody said it was a *great* vacation!

Was I there? Did I take the same vacation? Lou Ellen wondered.

On Lou Ellen and Burt's subsequent three- or four-day weekend trips to Valley Lake to camp and fish or to work on the property, Kevin sometimes went along to help Burt do some of the projects. After one such trip, just before leaving to return to Florida, Kevin was riding with Lou Ellen, following Burt in his truck, which Burt was planning to leave at the garage after he ran some other errands. Burt stopped first at a convenience store, and as they were leaving the store, Kevin pointed to the truck and said to Lou Ellen, "Father the follow!" Of course they laughed about his tangled tongue.

About five miles down the road, Kevin unintentionally said something else backward, and it started to get funnier. Then they stopped with Burt to eat lunch, and Kevin wanted Lou Ellen to tell him something that he didn't want Burt to hear.

"Tell me, Mom, and don't let Dad hear ... whisper in my eye!" Kevin said.

"You probably could hear it better if I whispered in your *ear*, Kevin," she said, laughing so hard her sides hurt. By now, they were both getting giddy, and *everything* was starting to be too funny.

Lou Ellen and Kevin got into the truck with Burt to run one more errand, and they stopped at a service station to get gas. Burt got out and was checking under the hood, at which point Kevin dared Lou Ellen to honk the horn. With her history of dare taking, *of course* she did it! Burt nearly jumped out of his skin *and* bumped his head! Kevin and Lou Ellen were laughing hysterically, and Burt got sorely aggravated with them, which made them laugh even harder ... until tears rolled down both their faces. Then Kevin, *still* with tangled tongue, said, "Mom, this is the first time I have ever *cried* until I *laughed!*" They both hopelessly lost it at that point, and Burt had absolutely no choice but to join in the laughter too. *Had Burt not known better, he would have declared we had been "taking a nip" or had finished a whole bottle,* Lou Ellen thought.

During the next couple of years after their infamous and unforgettable vacation, Kevin and Ryan loved to take a week of "rest and recreation" at the same time and go to Valley Lake to camp out together. Burt had replaced the small motor home with a camper that was much roomier, and Lou Ellen had also rented a three-bedroom house and partially furnished it—just a mile from the property—to use when they took their frequent trips there and to live in during the time they would be building their retirement home. Then she unintentionally moved from Cape Canaveral into the rental house six months before Burt was completely retired because they kept extending his retirement date. They were closing his division of the company, but they needed him until it was complete.

When Kevin and Ryan were taking their "just brothers" vacation together, they slept in the camper and went to the rented house for meals, showers, etc. They said their main objective was to help their parents get rid of the unwanted and destructive critters that had homesteaded on the land. Truthfully, Lou Ellen knew they just wanted to hunt, fish, and play their Wild West games because they always rented the movie *Tombstone* to watch. Kevin sometimes brought Jennifer and Evan with him if they were on break from year-round school; therefore, Lou Ellen enjoyed spending time with her grandchildren while Kevin and Ryan played. They all remembered those times as the most fun times they had there. Lou Ellen thought the boys actually enjoyed those times better before they built their home, as it was a little wilder then. For various reasons, those days had been some of the most memorable to Burt and her as well.

CHAPTER TWENTY-SIX

While Lou Ellen had numerous happy memories, she still remembered the last years of her mother's and daddy's lives. She was at peace about that period in her life, and she currently understood a lot that she hadn't at the time.

Even after Lou Ellen was married and moved away, she could never please her mother. She and Burt had always shared with her daddy and mother some of what they knew were God's material blessings. Through the years, among other things, they had given them their first automatic washing machine, floor fan, microwave, freezer, television, and even the last automobile they owned.

After they moved from Colorado Springs to Cape Canaveral, Lou Ellen occasionally drove to Cloverton alone just to spend time with them for a few days. Her mother loved curly perms, so she always took one with her and curled her hair. Her daddy loved her cooking, so she cooked his favorite foods. Her mother had a green thumb and usually had a beautiful hanging plant she was really proud of. Lou Ellen would admire it and tell her how beautiful it was, because growing pots of flowers was the only thing her mother really loved to do.

When Lou Ellen started packing the car to leave for the trip back home, her mother would insist that she take the plant home with her. If she took it, her mother then complained to the neighbor.

"Lou Ellen took my purty flowers home with her." She didn't bother to tell her neighbor she had insisted that Lou Ellen take it. When Lou Ellen heard about it later, she would refuse to take it the next time.

"Mother, I don't want to take your plant; it looks great right where it hangs," she'd say.

But her mother then would tell the neighbor lady, "I offered it to Lou Ellen, but she wouldn't take it. It's not good enough for her." Lou Ellen vowed she would stop trying to please her. But she didn't.

Sometimes when she went back to visit, the plant would be gone. When she inquired about it, her mother would say, "Somebody stole it." Lou Ellen was rather certain she had given it to someone else, since nothing except the plant was ever missing. Eventually she came to realize that she would never be able to do enough to earn her mother's love. While she continued to help them, she finally accepted that there were some things in a person's life one could never change, and that was one of hers. She just continued to do what her heart led her to do.

At least once a year, Lou Ellen drove to Cloverton to bring her parents back to visit in her home for a week, and she almost always brought them to stay during the Christmas season every year as well. After Granny Simpson passed away, her mother always came with her daddy because she didn't want to stay home alone. She and Burt had taken them to all the tourist attractions in the surrounding areas, including Kennedy Space Center, Disney World, and Sea World. Cypress Gardens was her mother's favorite place to go because it consisted of magnificent trees, acres of exotic plants, and beautiful flowers of all species. At one point, it was one of Florida's biggest attractions, because in addition to the botanical gardens, it featured a water ski show, Southern belle models, performing birds, and many other entertaining shows.

Lou Ellen was extremely concerned about her daddy and mother's eating habits, especially when her daddy was sick … and after they got older. When he came out of his depression, she hadn't worried because he always cooked well for them. By then she had found a doctor her daddy liked and trusted, who could get him started on his medicines, and he didn't have to go back to the institution any more. Until the medicine started working and he leveled out, he had periods of disinterest in most everything, including food. Her mother always asked him what she should cook.

"Nothing much. I'll just eat corn flakes," he often replied. He knew she didn't like to cook anyway, so they just ate things that were already processed and didn't even have to be heated. Once her mother had opened a can of corned beef hash and ate some from the can without heating it. Afterward she had just put the remainder in the refrigerator—still in the can and uncovered. Lou Ellen was constantly worried about the possibility that they would get food poisoning.

At her home Lou Ellen cooked and baked a lot, and she began to cook extra. She made and then froze a lot of TV dinners to take to her mother and daddy at least every other month. She and Burt bought them a microwave and showed them how to use it. In the beginning her daddy had used it, and they had eaten the TV dinners. Her mother, however, never learned how to use it. When her daddy was not mentally well enough to handle the food preparation, they just ate boxes of cereal and bags of cookies, peanut butter, and cheese. They ate all the cakes and desserts Lou Ellen had baked and put into their freezer, but the healthy TV dinners were left in the freezer.

Lou Ellen's daddy never talked to her about her biological mother until his later years, and then only when he was in the gregarious stage of one of his episodes. His comments were always in bits and pieces, at times making no sense at all. Therefore, she was never sure if what he was saying was real or imagined. But when he was well, it was as though her birth mother had never existed, and he didn't want to talk about her at all. He did confirm some of the stories about the day she'd left Lou Ellen and Nathan alone—about the wreck, the soldier's demise, and her mother's facial scars. Lou Ellen often wondered if it was too painful for him to talk about, so she was afraid to ask questions and possibly upset him. On one occasion her daddy also confirmed that Lou Ellen looked exactly like her mother, which some of his sisters and other relatives had already told her.

As the years passed and Lou Ellen's mother and daddy got older, her daddy couldn't take care of himself or Lena the way he had before, and he didn't drive much anymore. Lena would call the ambulance to come get her for one of her imaginary ailments, which took her to the hospital where they would check her out and find nothing wrong. They then called her brother to come get her because Lou Ellen didn't live close enough. The next week or two, Lena would repeat the same routine. With Lena's consent, her family finally put her in Shady Acres Manor, a nursing home thirty miles away in Valley Lake. Lou Ellen drove to Cloverton to talk to her daddy about moving to Cape Canaveral to live with her and Burt. He said he didn't want any part of a nursing home.

"Daddy, will you come live with Burt and me?"

"I'll go stay till Lena gets well enough to come home," he replied. And they packed up his clothes and drove to Florida.

Daniel never complained while he was living with Lou Ellen and Burt, but he was eager to go to see his wife as often as Lou Ellen offered. They lived seven or eight hours away, and she worked all week. She rearranged her schedule at work, took Fridays off every other weekend, and took her daddy to see Lena. Her parents' furniture and other belongings were still in the rented house in Cloverton, so Lou Ellen and her daddy stayed there when she took him back to visit. Each day they drove thirty miles to Shady Acres Manor and back, so Daniel could visit with Lena.

Her daddy knew it was hard on her to make that trip to Cloverton and work full-time too, but he wanted to be with his wife. For the first time in her life Lou Ellen saw her mother hug him and appear happy to see him when they went to visit.

Back home with Lou Ellen, he wrote Lena letters telling her she would get better soon, and they would go home again. But Lena repeatedly said she loved it there in Shady Acres Manor, which was understandable—she received a lot of attention and had zero responsibilities. Though he didn't complain, Lou Ellen knew her daddy was just patiently waiting to be reunited with Lena. Three months passed.

"Daddy, have you thought about going to Shady Acres to live with Mother?" Lou Ellen asked her daddy one day. He appeared to give it some thought, and finally he looked up at her.

"Yeah, that'll be all right for the time being…just until she gets better, and we can go back home."

Lou Ellen took him back for another visit and initiated the paperwork process, but it took a couple of weeks for interviews and paperwork to be done and other technicalities. It finally came to pass. In the beginning her daddy and mother were in separate rooms, but in a short time they were able to get a room together.

A couple of months later, along with Jeremy and Sue's help, Lou Ellen and Burt gave a surprise birthday party for her daddy at the nursing home, and most of his relatives came. He thoroughly enjoyed the afternoon and entertained them with his harmonica.

After Lou Ellen and Burt moved to Valley Lake and built a home on their retirement property, they often took her daddy and mother out for a day. They took them on a drive back to

Cloverton for a visit or out to their own property to fish and see all the flowers. And they always brought them to their home for holidays.

For a little while both her daddy and mother seemed happy and all was well, but it didn't last. Before long, her daddy got too much attention from the nurses, CNAs, social worker, etc. to please Lena. Because he was a people person, he went out of their room to talk to other residents, and he blew the harmonica for the activities hour. Soon her mother became jealous and complained he left her alone all the time.

A jealous person can make all kinds of trouble, and her mother did it all. Lou Ellen was called constantly for one problem or another. Eventually her mother apparently decided invalids got more attention; so she got a wheelchair and stopped walking.

Daniel pushed Lena to the dining room, to activities, and anyplace she wanted to go ... until he fell and broke his hip. Then he never walked again. For a short time, Lena maneuvered her wheelchair herself but soon abandoned it for the bed. She said the nurses told her not to get up because she might fall, which they denied. Finally, she said she couldn't walk at all.

One night while at the nursing home looking after her daddy and mother, Lou Ellen left to go home but had forgotten her sweater and went back to get it. As she entered their room, her mother was walking across the room to the sink. Lena would do whatever it took to get attention, and lying in bed pretending to be an invalid got her plenty of attention in the nursing home.

Lou Ellen often took her daddy and mother home-cooked food for supper. One night, she took their food, took care of any complaints they had with the CNAs, cleaned their dentures, and went back to the nurses' station to talk to the nurse. Her mother apparently thought Lou Ellen had left for the night, and as Lou Ellen came close to the door on her way back, she heard her mother loudly complaining to her daddy in the same condescending voice Lou Ellen remembered as a child.

"Lou Ellen thinks nobody can't do nothin' but *her!*"

By then Lou Ellen had long known she would go to her own grave never having been able to please Lena no matter what she did. So she could recall that incident had actually made her mad, more than it had hurt. She had only been trying to help make things better for them, and she felt she was wasting her valuable time.

One of Lena's own relatives told Lou Ellen that Lena talked to Daniel in her raised voice in hateful, disdainful tones all the time and that she was just an unhappy person. If Daniel started having too much to do with anyone or liking any one too much, even Lena's own relatives, she began criticizing that person to him, finding fault with any and everything about them in order to make him dislike them. One of Lena's most successful ploys was to tell Daniel that a particular person had verbally mistreated her. As Lou Ellen was growing up, she had thought Lena just didn't love *her*. Eventually she came to the realization that her mother didn't seem to be able to love anybody and didn't want to share Daniel's love for her with any other person either.

Lou Ellen regretted that she could not change the circumstances of her daddy and mother's situation. It was an utterly helpless feeling she never mastered. Even in later years, Lena made it clear she resented that Lou Ellen could talk her daddy into going to the doctor and could get him to take his medicines, but *she* couldn't. Yet every time he became sick, her mother always called her.

To Lou Ellen, her mother was an enigma. In one sense she was a child in a woman's body who needed love too, and in the other sense she could be a devious and mean-spirited adult. Lena certainly had Daniel's love, but it seemed she was never able to share that love without feeling threatened. Lou Ellen never saw Lena return his love in any form or fashion either. Still, he doted on her to the end.

There came a time when Lou Ellen finally realized that her mother was a victim too. Truthfully, she felt sad for how miserable her mother must have been. *We can all have our demons, whether they are great or small, real or imagined. Whether they are demons of fear, insecurity, pride, jealousy, or any others, they can still be demons, and each of us handles them in our own way,* she thought. Her mother's fears and insecurities were fueled by the inconsistencies of Daniel's illness, just as hers had been. They'd just handled them differently. Her mother was not a strong person, and it was easier for her to give up and let others care for her. She'd never known anything else.

Eventually inactivity was Lena's worst enemy. She must have enjoyed being sick, being coddled and attended to, and lying on the bed prostrate. She seemed to be happy there. Maybe she had convinced herself she really was helpless. She had always been like the little boy who cried wolf, so when she became ill with a cold and flu symptoms, it apparently progressed to pneumonia, which went undetected. She died suddenly one night shortly after telling the nurse she was "feeling some better."

Lou Ellen's consolation about her mother's death was her memory of an incident that happened a few months before Lena went to the nursing home. She called her mother and daddy every Sunday to check on them. One Sunday, her mother told her she had been *saved* through a popular televised evangelistic program. Lou Ellen told her that it was great news. She truly hoped and prayed that her mother had sincerely made that decision to live eternally with God.

Daniel was heartbroken and took Lena's death hard. Lou Ellen prayed and asked God to comfort him, and she and Burt took turns staying all night in a recliner beside his bed for nearly a week until he began to improve. She asked God to allow her daddy and her to have a little time together to enjoy a real father and daughter relationship, and he answered her prayers again. Her daddy lived another five years, and they were both able to express their love for each other and had some memorable times together. Sometimes she and Burt had taken him out to their property and fished together in one of their ponds. Daniel fished from his wheelchair while Burt baited his hooks and removed the fish he caught.

Additionally, Daniel told Burt many times how much he loved him and appreciated all he and Lou Ellen had done for Lena and him through the years and were still doing for him. Lou Ellen had spent years not knowing his true feelings, not realizing just how much love he felt inside. He may not have been a demonstrative person, but he didn't have the freedom to show it around Lena, even if he had been. She came to realize that, like she and Burt's mom had talked about years ago, her daddy was one of the people who had felt love all those years but couldn't show it outwardly for whatever reason. *I have just described myself when Burt entered my life,* Lou Ellen thought. *I had not had any practice.* Maybe her daddy had just never learned how, but she chose to believe that during his last five years, she and Burt taught him by example.

Her daddy and her brother mended their relationship and were much closer too. Nathan, who was also in poor health and lived in the Midwest, visited several times before their daddy passed away. He told Lou Ellen he understood that their daddy had been ill all those years and couldn't control his mental condition and actions. They both felt that if they had known as much about the illness then as they eventually came to know, perhaps they could have kept him on a medicine that would have prevented the severe mood swings, and he could have led a relatively normal life. During those visits, Lou Ellen got to know her brother better and came to realize what a tender heart he had.

A memory that baffled Lou Ellen for a long time was one of a statement her daddy made while she and Burt were in the process of building their home and before her mother died. She had gone to Shady Acres to take him and her mother for an afternoon drive around town to see the azaleas and other flowers blooming, which her mother loved to do. Then she took them to see the progress being made on the house.

"I'm proud for y'all. I just hope you don't lose it," her daddy said.

"Lose it? I don't know what you mean … it is ours, Daddy. We can't lose it," she said. But he didn't say anything more.

Lou Ellen had not understood that statement at the time, but now she knew what he meant. All those years ago when his health was good and he'd had steady work, he had sometimes bought an older used car, new lawn mower, new plow, or a mule to work his garden plots. She remembered that every time he got sick and was taken to the institution for several weeks or months, everything he owned was gone when he came home. His mule for gardening was either sold or given back to whomever he'd bought it from, his pigs and chickens were gone, as well as his automobile—if he'd had one. Sometimes even his garden produce had wasted, and the garden plot had succumbed to the weeds. Everything he had worked hard for and accomplished was gone. He always had to start all over again. That alone would have been enough to severely depress most people. Lou Ellen was sure it depressed him too, but she never once heard her daddy complain.

Without the perpetual negative influence he had always lived with, Daniel's mental health improved and remained mostly stable for the remainder of his life, and his memory was unbelievable for all he had endured during his lifetime. Burt and Lou Ellen often couldn't think of a person's name or of the place where a certain incident had occurred, and one of them would say, "Let's ask Pop," which is what they often called him in his latter years. When they asked, invariably he would bow his head, blink really fast for a few seconds, and then come up with the name or place. Lou Ellen asked him to write down all the names of his fourteen brothers and sisters by age and as much as he could remember about all of them, and he did. But she never asked about her biological mother. She didn't know if his wound was still as severe as hers once had been, and she couldn't take the chance that she might cause him pain.

Daniel never read a note of music, but he was gifted with musical talent. Early in his life he had taught himself to blow a harmonica and to play the piano and organ "by ear." The only music he truly loved was Southern gospel. During his last few years he had no interest in TV, so she and Burt kept him supplied with harmonicas, gospel CDs, and a continuous-play CD player. Often a CD repeated the same songs around the clock, changed only when Lou Ellen or Burt arrived to feed him supper. The music also served to help drown out other sometimes unpleasant noises in the nursing home, and he slept better. Though bedridden, he was content and never complained. Day after day, he blew his harmonica along with the music on the CDs, and the nurses told Lou Ellen sometimes they heard his harmonica during the night. Until his last year, when he no longer had the breathing ability and strength, he completely wore out a harmonica every three or four months—blowing it along with the music of the Chuck Wagon Gang, the Kingston Trio, the Florida Boys, and many more.

Every day for five years, Lou Ellen made sure her daddy had soft, home-cooked food for supper. It wasn't because the food served at the nursing home wasn't good, but because a lot of it was not anything Daniel had ever liked. He loved all soft vegetables, but did not like sandwiches, pizza, spaghetti, hot dogs, or hamburgers and couldn't chew fried meats that had not been simmered in gravy until fork-tender. As the years passed, he developed Parkinson's disease, and his hand was not steady enough to feed himself; so Lou Ellen fed him. She kept a variety of individual servings of food he liked frozen and handy. She eventually hired a lady to help two days every week and when they went on their annual vacation. Lou Ellen took Daniel's food to the helper to keep in her freezer, so all she had to do was heat it and feed him.

Burt was a tremendous help to her too, and he often went with her every night to feed Daniel. Burt's gift of merriment and encouragement was irresistible and contagious. Her daddy would laugh and talk with Burt and cut up to the point Lou Ellen couldn't get him to stop laughing long enough to eat. Sometimes she shooed Burt down the hall to entertain *other* residents until she finished feeding her daddy. Additionally, Burt often went alone to feed him for her, sometimes just to give Lou Ellen a break or other times when out of town girlfriends came to visit. She could then relax and be free to spend time with them. When Lou Ellen went alone to feed him, invariably, her daddy's first words were, "How's Burt?" She knew Daniel dearly loved Burt, and he missed him when he didn't come.

When they were together, Burt and Daniel constantly teased each other. Her daddy teased Burt about the times when he and Lou Ellen were dating and sat in the car in the driveway for a while after they got home.

"I bet you didn't know I was peekin' at y'all through the cracks in the bedroom wall, did you? I was making sure you were behavin' out there!" her daddy said.

Of course Burt played along and said, "Pop, I can't *believe* you were watching us all that time. Man! It's a good thing I *did* behave; you had a shotgun!"

Her daddy loved to tease and to laugh, and he did a lot of both. He had the perfect person to practice with.

A particularly favorite story her daddy loved to tell was of the time two of his teenage sisters had a tube of lipstick. He sneaked it, put hot sauce all over it, and hid to watch them put it on. Then laughing hysterically, he ran for his life. While telling the story, he always got tickled all over again. Through his last few years, he told it repeatedly. Like scripted dialogue, it never varied.

"Did grandmother whip your behind for that?" Lou Ellen always asked.

"No," was always his terse reply.

"Well, she *should* have!" she would exclaim with feigned disapproval. And her daddy would laugh even more.

One day Lou Ellen complained to her daddy about the deer eating her flowers.

"I am so tired of my flowers just disappearing. They can eat a whole flowerbed in one night."

"Well, *they* have to eat too," he said.

"But not my flowers, Daddy. I am so mad! I hope they get diarrhea!" she replied.

They had that same conversation often, and he always got tickled. He loved taunting her about the deer. Quite often when she went in the evenings to feed him, just to tease her, he would ask, "How's the deer?" And she would pretend outrage over something they had eaten, though a lot of the time her outrage was genuine.

Another story her daddy often told was one he had always teased Lena about while she was living. He said it was the first time she'd ever seen an armadillo. She'd been watering her plants on the back porch when the ugly critter walked across the yard. Her daddy said Lena went running to the door, yelling for him.

"Daniel! Daniel... quick! Come look! Yonder comes the *devil!*" she'd said.

He couldn't stop laughing when he told it. He said, "She was not joking... she was dead serious."

As time passed, Lou Ellen sensed when their roles began to reverse. Her daddy became the child, and she became the parent. He said things only a child would say. On more than one occasion when a heavyset nurse came into his room, he looked at Lou Ellen with a mischievous smile.

"Ask her when it's due," he'd pretend to whisper. But his voice was clearly audible to the entire room.

"Ask her what she's gonna name it," he would say at other times. There had been one or two who were pregnant, and he'd just assumed they all were.

"Shh! … Daddy! Don't say that … it's not nice!" Lou Ellen usually whispered back, and he would giggle like a little kid.

The week Lou Ellen's daddy went home to be with the Lord, he spent several days in the hospital. For three years they had known he had an enlarged heart, and his body accumulated fluids. Eventually he developed congestive heart failure. X-rays showed his heart had enlarged to the point it practically filled his entire chest, but her daddy repeatedly said he did not have an ache or pain anywhere, much to the amazement of his doctor and the medical staff.

After a fashion, he sang gospels songs over and over to the nurses, and he sang even if no one was listening. Eventually he went into a deep sleep and never woke up. Lou Ellen was so thankful that God took him that way, without pain or difficulty breathing, as she had been told was a real possibility in light of his heart condition. God was so good! And she focused on that fact as she grieved his passing. She said her good-byes, knowing that one day they would be together again in heaven, and that her daddy would be healed in body *and mind.*

CHAPTER TWENTY-SEVEN

Every fall Burt and Lou Ellen took a vacation to celebrate Burt's birthday. In September, 2001, as previously planned, they flew to the Burlington, Vermont area for a week, along with Jeff and Nina, their friends from Cape Canaveral. They rented a car for the week and had plans to drive into Canada and New York while there. Lou Ellen had been slightly under the weather with a sore throat when they left Valley Lake and had been to the doctor and given antibiotics. After they arrived in Vermont, she continued to get sicker, had laryngitis, and was concerned about the possibility of ear problems when the time came to board the plane to fly home on Friday.

Therefore, Tuesday morning, on their way driving toward Canada, they stopped by a walk-in clinic for Lou Ellen to see a doctor. While awaiting her turn to be seen, the receptionist was watching television and announced that a small airplane had just crashed into one of the twin towers in New York. No one showed undue concern; accidents happen. A few minutes later, she said another plane had crashed into the tower, this time a passenger plane. Of course all the patients started watching the TV and heard that both of the planes were large planes, and authorities suspected it was a terrorist attack.

When she went into the examination room to see the doctor, Lou Ellen asked Burt to go with her. Burt had always been well blessed with the gift of gab—not necessarily an asset *that* day. It seemed Burt and the doctor talked about everything imaginable—from careers, to traveling, to gardening—to the point the doctor stopped his exam and just stood and talked to Burt. Lou Ellen sat on the table thinking about Jeff and Nina waiting in the car, and she got antsy and more frustrated by the minute.

Then the doctor had a phone call that he said he had been waiting for and just *had* to take. He apologized and left the room. As soon as he walked out, Lou Ellen looked at Burt.

"When he comes back, *do not* say a word to him so we can get out of here!" she said.

They waited ten minutes, and the moment the doctor walked back into the room, she *could not* believe her ears!

"Doc, have you ever been to Branson?" Burt asked. And off they went on another sightseeing trip, and there she sat ... waiting! If body language and looks could have killed, Burt would have been ancient history.

Lou Ellen finally got a prescription for medicine, and by the time they got back to the car where Jeff and Nina were waiting, it had been announced on the radio that the Canadian border was closed and all planes were grounded. In other words, no planes would be arriving or departing until further notice. But at that point they still weren't overly concerned about their flights home.

Lou Ellen told Jeff and Nina what had happened with Burt in the doctor's office, and they all had a good laugh. They had been to Branson with Jeff and Nina on their annual trip two years earlier, and the four of them had a memorable, fun-filled week there. But Lou Ellen had not particularly wanted to re-live them in that doctor's office.

Still unaware of the magnitude of the terrible disaster and senseless loss of so many lives that was occurring, they decided to sightsee and have lunch before going back to the condo to watch the news coverage on television. They stopped at a scenic water-fall, where they had to walk a long wooden bridge to the falls. A few tourists were already around the falls when they arrived. A gregarious lady there initiated a conversation with Burt—or perhaps it was Burt who initiated it—and they kept talking and talking.

Finally Lou Ellen said to Jeff and Nina, "If we start back across the bridge, maybe Burt will get the hint that we are ready to eat, stop talking, and follow us." They started out. About halfway on the bridge, they heard that tourist lady say to Burt, "Have you ever been to Branson?"

"Uh-uh! Say no! Say no!" Lou Ellen wanted to scream to Burt. *I must be dreaming! Twice in one day!* she thought. But they just laughed their way on across the bridge to the car—to wait for Burt. Of course the word Branson would always be Burt's bane. Any time Lou Ellen and their friends waited while Burt talked to someone else, she or one of their friends would invariably say, "Oh, I hope they've *never* been to *Branson!*"

They stopped at a restaurant for lunch that was supposed to be known for its good hamburgers. Burt looked at the menu, mentioned the mushroom burger sounded great, and ordered one. It took quite a while before the waitress brought their food, and when it came, Burt was shocked. He had a bun, mushrooms, lettuce, and tomato...and no meat! A Kodak moment! For a meat and potatoes man, that was just not acceptable. They kept reminding him he ordered "a *mushroom* burger," and that it must be exactly what they *meant* in that part of the country. After much teasing, he called the waitress over and asked her about the meatless burger. She was profusely apologetic, said it was a mistake, and brought him another burger—*with* the meat.

They spent most of the next two days of their vacation in the condo glued to the TV, concerned that their flights home had been canceled for good. Nina began calling car rental agencies, which were inundated with phone calls. Most of them had absolutely nothing available to rent; however, due to her perseverance, Nina eventually found a car to reserve.

On Friday morning they called the airlines again to check on their flights. They were told that all were still on the schedule, but the airport could not guarantee the planes would definitely depart. They were informed to be at the airport three hours in advance. At that point they had to decide if they should cancel

the car rental reservation or keep it in case their flights were canceled. After waiting two hours at the airport, their flights seemed
to remain promising, and Nina canceled the car reservation.

Jeff and Nina's flight was delayed, but eventually they made
the trip to Cape Canaveral without incident. Burt and Lou
Ellen's flight to Atlanta departed fairly close to schedule, and
they made that leg of the trip fine. But the flight from Atlanta to
Louiston was touch and go. Literally! They boarded, but according to the pilot, the plane had a "mechanical problem." They sat
stationary while it was corrected. The pilot finally came on the
intercom and told them the problem was solved, and their plane
departed an hour late. A few minutes later, the pilot's voice came
over the intercom.

"Ladies and gentlemen … we have a problem."

Words could not describe the instant fear Lou Ellen felt. She
knew the blood drained from her face! She knew the "mechanical problem" had to be back. Or worse yet, there was a bomb on
board … or a hijacker, or both! It was only a few seconds before
the pilot explained, but it was long enough for fear to momentarily paralyze her.

"Our landing gear will not retract. We can't fly to Louiston
like this, so we are going back and board another plane. Then we
will continue our flight to Louiston."

They eventually arrived safely in Louiston, collected their
vehicle, and drove on home to Valley Lake. Lou Ellen thought
about kissing the ground when they arrived in Valley Lake.
Instead, she said, "Thank you, dear Lord, for your love and protection this day … this week."

In spite of the atrocities recorded in American history that
week, they had many good memories of the trip.

CHAPTER TWENTY-EIGHT

While Burt watched an old western movie, Lou Ellen sat re-reading a novel she had read years ago, a story spanning decades and written in an Australian setting. Burt's movie ended, and he got up to get ready for bed.

"I'm calling it a night. Are you going to read a while?" he asked.

"Yes, but I'm kind of tired too, so I probably won't read long," she said, getting up to make a cup of hot cocoa.

"Have I told you yet today how much I love you?" Burt asked as he put his arms around her.

"Umm ... only twice so far ... maybe you're getting senile?" she teased, chuckling.

"I'll *never* get so senile I can't remember to tell you that I love you ... but I may repeat myself a lot. You are the best thing that ever happened to me. I just want you to always remember that," he said with a totally serious face.

"You have it all backward! *You* are the best thing that ever happened to *me!*" she said. "Have you forgotten about my life before you came into it?"

"I haven't forgotten *anything* about you and me, and I don't have anything backward. *You are* my life, and I love you *so* much. I just wish I could open up my heart and you could look inside and *see* what I *feel*—all the love I feel for you.

"Oh ... honey! I've always known that. *I* can feel it too. I don't need to see it. I love you just as much, so I know how it feels."

"Just wanted to be sure," he said, hugging her tight.

They kissed goodnight, and he strode off to bed, yawning.

With her cup of cocoa, she settled down with her book again, which brought to mind some more of her family's experiences. With Burt's job, they had often visited or lived far and wide—in places such as Spain, Africa, New Zealand, Hawaii, and Australia.

This book was bringing back memories of their experiences when they'd lived in "the land down under" Australian continent, out in the middle of the desert.

They'd lived in an oasis, a nice well-maintained one-mile-square village; but for the most part, the miles and miles of barren landscape were only broken by an occasional tiny settlement of two or three buildings that was inhabited by a sheep farmer and his family. The locals referred to those settlements as "sheep stations."

The water for their village was piped in from the Murray River 300 miles away in the city of Adelaide, and a water filter was an absolute necessity. After filling the bathtub with water once and seeing the sediment, everyone opted for showers in the future. For two years their temporary home was large, American manufactured, had all the necessities, and they were comfortable and happy. The village had a hospital that was sufficient—though not overly staffed.

Shopping for groceries could take half a day, because each shop was specialized—one for milk, one for produce, a bread store, a meat store and so on. There was always a long queue in each store, as well as the bank, where American money had to be converted to Australian money before going shopping for the groceries. Everyone learned what days the freshest produce and other supplies were delivered to the village, which accounted for even longer queues.

As with all parents, Burt and Lou Ellen had some tense, scary, and stressful situations involving their children, and some of theirs had happened while they were living in Australia. They had to travel the 300 miles to Adelaide every six weeks for orthodontist appointments for their oldest son, Kevin. About thirty miles of the road to Adelaide were unpaved and rugged, but it seemed more like one hundred miles since they could only drive about thirty miles an hour. They always drove to Adelaide on

Thursdays for Kevin's appointment on Fridays and spent the weekend shopping for things they couldn't buy in the outback. When *anyone* from their village went to Adelaide, they usually had a long list of items other villagers asked them to bring back. Current hit music records were popular items always in demand.

If it was dark when they went home on Sunday nights, they often had to stop on the dirt road going across the desert and wait for kangaroos to get off the road before they could continue driving. Honking the horn didn't seem to faze their little brains. The Aussies had sturdy "roo bars" on the front of their vehicles to prevent major damage to their radiator and other parts, in the event they hit a kangaroo. Understandably so; Lou Ellen thought they drove way too fast! Burt had shipped their American car to Australia, so *it* didn't have that protection.

Since the Aussies drive on the opposite side of the road than Americans, their car steering wheel, brakes, etc. were on the opposite side of their autos as well. So driving in large cities in an American car was somewhat of a challenge, particularly at major, multiple-lane intersections. Therefore, Burt and Lou Ellen decided the family would generally always take a bus to travel around the city after they drove to their rented flat.

One day they were waiting for their bus at a busy intersection, which had two lanes near the curb, designated just for buses. There were numerous buses arriving and departing simultaneously. They had to be careful to read the destination of each of the buses, but it was located high above the windshield. Lou Ellen and Burt saw the bus they needed approaching and stepped down next to the curb. They looked around to make sure Kevin and Ryan were beside them, but Ryan was gone! Lou Ellen panicked as a cold, paralyzing fear overcame her, but Burt went into action. He jumped on the bus nearest them and called his name, and there Ryan was! He had impulsively boarded the wrong bus. Except for their normal routes, she and Burt didn't know the city well enough to know where to begin looking for Ryan if they hadn't found him, and she felt sure Ryan wouldn't have known the address to tell anyone where he had boarded the wrong bus.

"Oh, dear God, thank you, thank you!" It was all Lou Ellen could remember saying.

Another bad scare they'd had in Australia happened with Kevin, who was seventeen years old at the time. He had a ten-speed bike, had been out riding, and had an accident on the way home. He walked into the kitchen and sat down at the dining table, obviously not feeling well. He told Lou Ellen and Burt he had a headache, that he had hit a rough place in the sidewalk concrete and flipped over the handlebars of the bike. Pushing the hair back from his forehead, they saw he had an enormous goose egg on his forehead, and upon further investigation saw that both of his pupils were completely dilated. Again that indescribable fear engulfed Lou Ellen. They lived only two houses away from the hospital, and they took him there immediately. He was admitted, kept overnight, and watched carefully. He recovered just fine, and she knew that was just one more of the numerous blessings from God.

And God looked out for the Newmans far more than they were even aware of at times.

One night Lou Ellen spent several hours walking the floor with a severe stomachache and then threw up. She woke Burt, who took her to the hospital where she was kept overnight and given a morphine shot for pain. The next morning they told her she'd only had a severe case of indigestion, but that she should go to see Dr. Angela Cook the following week. She did, and Dr. Cook ordered x-rays.

When she went back for the follow-up, Dr. Cook told her the x-rays looked fine to her, but she was sending them to Adelaide for a radiologist to read to be on the safe side. She said she would call if anything turned up. But Lou Ellen knew she was fine if the doctor couldn't see anything herself.

Two months later, after she'd been on a strict diet for several days to lose five pounds, Lou Ellen and Burt went out to dinner on Saturday night to celebrate her reaching her weight goal, and she ate a delicious lobster tail. That night she was up all night with a severe stomachache, to the point of throwing up again. However, she didn't wake Burt to take her to the hospital until morning. She didn't want to spend another night in the hospital, only to be told she'd had indigestion again! The doctor on duty that early Mother's Day Sunday morning just happened to be the surgeon, Dr. Rawlston, who was also trained in plastic surgery. He retrieved Lou Ellen's records, looked through them and found the x-rays from two months previous, and read the radiologist's report. The report said she had numerous tiny gallstones, and that she needed to see the surgeon right away. Dr. Rawlston explained the urgency; there was a chance that while passing through a bile duct, one tiny stone could possibly get lodged and therefore could complicate surgery. But somehow her x-rays had been filed away in her records without anyone contacting Dr. Rawlston *or* her. Dr. Rawlston wanted to perform surgery as quickly as possible.

The hospital there had a skeletal staff. The specialized doctors were rotated often, and they didn't even have an anesthesiologist on staff. If major surgery had to be done, it was usually done on one scheduled day of the week when an anesthesiologist from Adelaide came to the village. The other option was to have the surgery in Adelaide, but she chose to stay in the village. She wasn't yet convinced she needed surgery.

"Maybe they are not really *my* x-rays," Lou Ellen said. "Dr. Cook said mine looked okay... she couldn't *see* any gallstones."

Dr. Rawlston then took the x-rays out, put them up on the screen, and showed her and Burt exactly what the radiologist was talking about. But Lou Ellen questioned him right up through the time they sedated and wheeled her—groggy and still unsure—into surgery two days later.

"Doctor, I can see those are surely *somebody's* gallstones in those x-rays, but are you sure those are my x-rays?" she asked, slurring her words slightly. And they laughed at her.

During surgery, the surgeon could not feel the gallstones in the gallbladder; so he stopped the surgery and went out to talk to Burt. He explained the situation to him and said he still felt sure the gallbladder was diseased and was the cause of Lou Ellen's pain; and he wanted to remove it anyway. Of course Burt told him to do what he thought needed to be done. It was definitely a good thing she wasn't aware of that conversation taking place; she would've been totally convinced he had the wrong x-rays and would've gotten off the table and escaped!

Then Dr. Rawlston had to go back and scrub again and finish the surgery. He did find the many tiny gallstones after he removed the gallbladder, and later he told Lou Ellen he had saved some of them for her just to prove to her he had the right records! While she was not from Missouri, she really did need to be shown some proof that time. Those were pre-laparoscopic surgery days, but she had a well-crafted, paper-thin, six-inch scar for a souvenir, thanks to the surgeon's plastic surgery training.

One of Lou Ellen's most embarrassing experiences also happened in Australia. Burt told her they'd been invited to a party. It was going to be a barbecue, and it was located several miles out across the desert at one of the sheep stations. Burt and Lou Ellen and three other couples were going to ride together, sitting on lawn chairs in the back of a pickup with a camper shell. Lou Ellen did not ask any of the other ladies what they were going to wear because as far as she was concerned, it was a no-brainer: a jeans and T-shirt occasion. Unfortunately, she was the only one who thought so.

When the truck arrived to get Burt and Lou Ellen, she saw the other ladies were formally dressed ... as in floor-length gowns and heels. She could only surmise that after two years in the outback, those ladies were just dying to wear formals! However, it was held inside a building, rather than outside as she had expected. And there was music and dancing. She had not particularly enjoyed just sitting at the table all night, but she did. She refused to get up and dance and enter the best-dressed contest!

Regardless of the circumstances, they always managed to have fun. Going home, on the ride back across that vast desert in the land down under, far from their home in the USA, they were stopped at a railway crossing by a long train. They sat waiting for several minutes. Everyone was tired, and all was quiet when suddenly Burt burst out singing, "Pardon me, boys, is that the Chattanooga Choo-Choo?"

Smiling, she closed the Australian novel that she'd forgotten about and walked into the bathroom to prepare for bed.

CHAPTER TWENTY-NINE

At six a.m. Lou Ellen was up, sitting in her recliner drinking coffee, doing her Bible study and prayer time. She was thanking God for all he was to her, and yes, *even* thanking him for her childhood. She'd never spent a lot of time looking back and wishing things had been different. She felt it was a waste of her precious time. She had never been one to blame her failures or shortcomings on her childhood. And now she knew a person could remember both the good *and* the bad events, leave the bad ones behind, refuse to wallow in regrets, and then strive to make the present day the best that it could be. Like every human being alive, she'd made mistakes. She thought of a few major regrets and wished she could use her hindsight and wisdom to make young people aware of the pitfalls.

As a parent, she regretted that she didn't spend more quality time with her children when they were growing up. She loved them beyond measure, but she'd often been more concerned for their health, education, and physical needs than for their emotional and spiritual ones. She and Burt had given them the fundamentals and the foundation for their faith, while neglecting to make sure they stayed grounded in worship and fellowship with other Christians and stayed involved in church. She regretted the times when they'd allowed their children to be picked up by the church bus to attend Sunday school and church while she and Burt stayed home.

She and Burt always told them how much they loved them, but they could've *shown* them more. Now she knew that time is the most valuable possession parents can give their children. If only she had realized that then, and considering her own childhood, shouldn't she have? She regretted that she had not taught her children, by example, how to put God first in their lives. Yet, she was now ever so thankful to him that they grew up to be fine responsible young men, husbands, and fathers to her beautiful grandchildren. She was ever mindful of God's powerful hand in that.

Lou Ellen was in the kitchen baking chocolate chip cookies, which she sometimes did for part of her sharing ministry. Elderly ladies around town, as well as the office ladies at their former church, loved to see her coming to "sweeten the day."

She and Burt had gone to a church several miles from their home for ten years, but they had moved their membership to one closer to home just a few months ago. Pastor Neal was the pastor of their former church and had remained a good friend and mentor. Burt still shared his garden produce with him, and they often dropped by and visited with him.

The back door opened, and Burt stepped just inside the door.

"Honey, I came in to tell you I'll be gone for a little while," he said. "I just finished picking the squash and green beans, and I'm going to drop some off for the Wilsons, the Fords, and then take some to Pastor Neal."

"Oh, wait...I can take Pastor Neal's veggies when I take the ladies' cookies, and that'll save you a trip," she said. "I have to drop some cookies off for Mrs. Winnie at the nursing home too, so *I'll* be gone a little while also."

"Well...unless you want to have to go to the altar and repent on Sunday, you'd better take Pastor Neal some cookies too," Burt said, smiling.

"I know that's true! I just happen to have a couple in a bag with his name on it already. It'll be a little while before I go...I have to finish baking the rest of the cookies," she said.

An hour later, Lou Ellen arrived at her old church and passed through the foyer to the hallway that led to the church offices. Looking down the hall to the left she saw Pastor Neal in his office, talking on the phone. Down the hall to the right, Pam and Nicki were in Pam's office talking, so she joined them. They were happy to see her, and the three of them sat and talked for a little while as Pam and Nicki enjoyed the cookies. Lou Ellen saw Pastor Neal when he hung up the phone, so she stood and hugged them.

"Ladies, I have a busy day planned, so I'd better get moving. I'll drop the pastor's goodies off to him and be on my way. You two have a great day."

"Okay, thanks again for the sweets. We've missed you. Drop by more often, so we can talk longer," Pam said.

"Yes, those cookies are just what the doctor ordered...they hit the spot! It was good to see you again, Lou Ellen," Nicki said as she walked back into her own office and Lou Ellen walked down the hall.

Lou Ellen thought Pastor Neal was the calmest, most compassionate, and wisest man she'd ever known. He was past retirement age, but he said he had no plans to retire yet; he loved doing the Lord's work. He'd lost his wife to cancer a few years earlier and had a housekeeper who came to clean and cook his meals three days a week. Lou Ellen had talked with him at length on several occasions when they were members there. He knew everything about her past and was a spiritual mentor to her. And he'd often told her how much he appreciated Burt as a friend, as well as his encouraging and fun-loving personality. He and Burt teased each other unmercifully. Seeing her approach, Pastor Neal arose from his chair and greeted her warmly.

"Good morning, Mrs. Newman! Come in and have a seat. How *are* you this lovely day?"

"I'm fine, Pastor. I just dropped by with a bag of veggies Burt sent you, and a couple of calorie-free cookies I made," she replied, a smile tickling the corners of her mouth.

"Oh! Good! Thank him for me … but concerning the absence of calories … I suspect you are handling the truth just a mite carelessly, so you know you should probably go to the altar Sun—"

"I know … I know! Burt mentioned that already," Lou Ellen interrupted, grinning. "But he said if I *didn't* bring you some cookies, you'd make me go to the altar. I knew if I did bring you some, you'd fuss, as usual, about how I always try to fatten you up! So I guess I just can't win!"

"Well, confession is good for the soul!" he jovially replied, already chewing on a cookie.

For a few minutes they brought each other up to date on their families and discussed the upcoming events at both their churches. But then the conversation turned more serious.

"Lou Ellen, do you have something on your mind you need to talk about?" Pastor Neal asked.

"Umm … no, not really. Why do you ask, Pastor?"

"You just seem to be a little preoccupied today," he said. "And I sense you seem sort of pensive somehow. Your smile isn't quite as wide today."

Lou Ellen knew that if there was ever a person who could understand and who had the wisdom to advise her, it would be Pastor Neal. She could talk to Burt about *anything,* but he always had *her* best interest at heart. And she didn't want to worry him about something she wasn't even sure was a problem. She had never been one to bother others with her problems, but today she could use some advice in helping to understand what God might be asking of her.

"Pastor, I have had—do have—something on my mind. I could use help with it, but I know you are a very busy man. What's bothering me isn't even something I can voice in so many words … that in itself is part of the problem. I guess it's more of a *feeling* than anything."

"Oftentimes, just talking about it can clear that up for you and make you see the problem for what it is … or isn't. It might not even all come together the first time you talk about it; it might take several conversations to get to the bottom of it. It's worth a try, though."

"Okay, I will try. I am sure you remember I told you about my big mistake. Years ago I wandered away from God and did my own navigating, doing what *I* wanted to do. I was too busy furthering my education, working, raising my family, reaping all God's benefits and blessings, without ever stopping to consider that I was disobeying him or giving any thought to what I needed to be doing for him—"

"Yes, Lou Ellen, I remember. You called those your 'wasted years,' but you also told me you asked for God's forgiveness and that you know he has forgiven you. So you need to remember that God remembers your sin no more. He said it's as far removed as the east is from the west."

"That's true, I do remember that. Psalm 103 is one of my favorite books of the Bible. It's not that at all, because I've had peace in my heart about that for years; yet, lately I've had a relentless feeling that I'm not in his will. I've prayed about it many times, daily, as a matter of fact. But I still don't know exactly what his will for me is—what he wants me to do, if anything," she said.

"Lou Ellen, God is faithful. You have to be faithful too. You have to continue to pray. You have to fervently say, 'Lord, I turn my entire heart and life over to you. I will no longer hold back a tiny portion for myself; my heart is all yours ... do with me what you will. I trust you with my whole heart, and I will obey you,' and then I believe he will reveal to you whatever it is you are troubled by or need to do."

"Oh, Pastor, I have no intention of giving up. I know that it doesn't matter what service you do for him, even the most menial task ... from floor mopping ... to door locking ... to pastoring—and everything in between. I believe if your heart is right with him and you have the right attitude and motive, it's important to God."

"You're right, but you certainly don't want to limit God's blessings and provisions for you by a lack of faith and obedience. Keep praying."

They continued to talk for another ten minutes, and Pastor Neal prayed with her. He reminded her of his open-door policy and told her she was welcome to come back and talk to him as often as she felt the need. Lou Ellen couldn't exactly describe the feeling, but she felt lighter somehow when she left the Pastor's office. Peaceful.

That night, Lou Ellen purposely went out on the veranda to look for Little Red. It'd been at least six weeks since she'd seen him, so she felt he had moved on to new territories. At least that was what she chose to believe, rather than the alternative. A neighbor had told her they'd seen a red fox that'd been run over up on the highway from their house, but she didn't want to even think it was Little Red. Glancing up at the sky, she noticed it was a little cloudy, but the clouds were drifting fast. Earlier the weatherman had said it would be cloudy early then clearing and cooler later that night, but she was tired and wouldn't be out there long. Feeling slightly disappointed, she turned to go back inside. As she did, she glimpsed a shadow under the security light down by the birdfeeder. Stopping to look closely, she saw movement, then even *more* movement. Quickly picking up the night-vision goggles, she walked to the edge of the veranda and focused on the grass under the light. *What? Could it be?* She held her breath ... then almost squealed with joy! There, running around on the ground were two ... no, *three* tiny, furry kits with Mama and Little Red hovering around them! She was beyond thrilled. It took a whole bucket of willpower not to go wake Burt to tell him the good news. She knew he would be happy too, but it could wait until morning. *Lord, you know our every thought—the desires of our hearts—no matter how small. You are an awesome, God!* she thought. *Thank you.* And she sat down to watch for a while ... and began to contemplate.

Through the years, Lou Ellen had sometimes been asked why she never "found" her biological mother or hadn't even tried to locate her. She could never answer that question, other than to say she just never had the desire. She wasn't sure a person could consciously miss something they'd never had. She didn't know why, for sure, but she may have been afraid she would be rejected again. No one ever suggested or came right out and said, "Your mother just didn't love you, so she left." But as a child, it certainly hadn't taken the mind of Einstein to come to that conclusion herself, and to believe she was just ... *unlovable.*

Until Burt, she thought. *After he came into my life, Mom Newman lovingly fulfilled my every need for a mother.*

Lou Ellen also felt her biological mother had always known where she was or could find out how to contact her, especially after she had grown up. At that point she had to have known there would have been no repercussions from Daniel. So Lou Ellen felt in her heart that her mother simply didn't have the desire, either. *Now* she thought that was sad for both of them, but she believed if it had been in God's plan for her, he would have brought it about. And she was content with that.

She thought about how life has a way of punching a hole in the heart and letting the fear, pain, and sadness drain away, leaving plenty of room for the good things of life: love, laughter, joy, and contentment. It's really a person's choice. You can choose what kind of a day you're going to have by your attitude, and you can choose the things that fill your heart to capacity. She knew God had so blessed her life that she could never express or do enough to show her appreciation. He gave her a family that was precious to her and brought her tremendous pleasure, joy, and happiness. Her heart was full of only these good things—good memories. And she chose to let her heart overflow with them. When love abounds, there isn't room for anything else.

Even so, she knew that a person's past is as much a part of his or her character as magnolias, corn pone, and doodlebugs are a part of the Deep South. She used to say it wasn't—that one's past didn't matter—but that didn't make it so. She used to say her past was just a period she never wanted to remember again, and for a lot of years she was successful. She used to say her life only began at sixteen years of age. She used to say she never wanted to go back there—to that birthplace of unpleasant memories. But maturity has a way of changing a person's mind. While she didn't live in her same hometown, she lived in close proximity, and she felt she was actually *home*.

Remembering the past had helped her focus on what was important for her future. Somewhere, very early along life's way, she'd realized that obsessing over the color of a house as a teenager was silly and shallow. But it took longer to understand that it was what happened *inside* that house of color—or no color as it were—that mattered. It was the good lessons learned inside those four walls that are important and that last a lifetime and build character. It was about learning to care for others, like her daddy cared for the widow ladies and anyone else he thought was in need. It was about trusting God to provide one's needs and then sharing his blessings with others. It was about having a role model, a daddy who never questioned God even as he went through the darkest valleys. It was about unconditional love … loving someone so deeply that it didn't matter if they loved you back. You still loved *them* anyway.

And those thoughts made Lou Ellen realize anew that others needed to hear about the greatest love of all, that of knowing Jesus as their personal Savior. They needed to know about his unconditional love, available to all who would sincerely ask for forgiveness of their sins and invite him to live in their heart and change them—and would then walk in fellowship with him. She wished she could tell them that it was that simple! Since she wasn't a speaker, she didn't know how to go about sharing that good news, but she was sure that, like Pastor Neal told her, God would someday reveal his intended will for her. And she knew he would bring her *through* whatever he brought her *to,* a knowledge that gave her great peace. God, in his own timing, would speak to her heart.

Lou Ellen had absolutely no doubt that it was God's plan and by his divine intervention that she and Burt were together. They were soul mates! Another of her greatest regrets was for those years they had not put God *first* in their lives together as husband and wife. They had wandered away from God and lived a busy life, giving God only the time that was left over, which was often non-existent. They'd always thanked him daily for their food and other blessings; otherwise, they prayed when they had the need, and went to church when it was convenient, which was sporadic at best and for several years, not at all.

Most of all, they thanked God for not giving up on them, for leading them back on the right path, and forgiving them for trying to lead according to their own plans, instead of following him and his plans for them. For many years now, she and Burt had been putting God first: reading his Word and asking for his continued guidance. They prayed daily for God to reveal his will for them and to give them the wisdom to recognize it when he did. And they were striving to *obey.*

God takes good care of his own.

CHAPTER THIRTY

When Lou Ellen heard a cat squabble somewhere in the distance, she realized she had once again spent more time out there than she had intended. The clouds had cleared, and the full moon was a huge, luminous orb hanging high above the horizon as it showered the backyard in a surreal aura that she could only describe as *spiritual* ... God's marvelous creation. Little Red and his family had moved on. The weatherman was right. It *had* turned cooler. All the night creatures had quieted, as though it was time to rest their tired voices, but the silence was occasionally interrupted by a hoot owl in the forest as his eerie call reverberated through the thick, dark woods. She had been so immersed in her thoughts that she had not been aware how chilled she had become. She needed to go inside now, but she wanted to spend just another minute thanking God for all his blessings.

As she gazed into the spectacular starry universe, suddenly one bright streak of white light shot across the sky and seemed to scatter into a zillion little lights as it turned downward and raced toward what seemed to be its earthly destination. It wasn't the first time she'd seen a meteor and marveled at God's wonders. It probably wouldn't be the last. But this one touched her on a different level. This one *moved* her, stirred her deep inside her soul. *What if all those tiny lights each touched a house or a person? One tiny star could touch so many lives!* she thought.

It was at that moment that Lou Ellen knew what God wanted her to do. She felt it to the core of her being, as surely as if he were standing before her, speaking. It was her sign, her revelation! Her mission was to share Jesus's love with others, to tell others what he had done for her. If she could tell *her* story, touch just one life and make a difference, give hope and encouragement to a single person, she would. She'd never had a gift for speaking, but with God's help, she could write it all down. She would leave the rest to him. She would obey! With a calmness of spirit she hadn't felt in a long time, she thanked God for his love and protection and prayed for his guidance and wisdom.

She hadn't heard a sound, but she sensed Burt's presence, even before he placed the soft, cozy blanket about her shoulders and wrapped his warm arms around her in one of his all-encompassing, loving bear hugs.

"Are you having a bad night, sweetie?" Burt asked.

"Oh! Absolutely *not!* I've had a wonderful night," she replied, snuggling against him. "I have a marvelous idea. I can't wait to tell you all about it. I'm going to write a story! Maybe I'll go call my brother... my guess is *he* may also have a great story to tell. And how about you, Burt... do *you* have a story to tell, too?" she asked, hardly stopping for breath, her words tumbling out and her voice literally bubbling over with excitement.

"Wow, mine would surely be a hoot, honey," Burt quipped as he led her back across the veranda, through the double doors, and into the welcoming warmth of their bedroom.